You Can't Bury Death

by

Peggy Doviak

A Magnolia Hill Mystery

Copyright Notice
This is a work of fiction. Names, characters, places, and incidents are either the product of the author's imagination or are used fictitiously, and any resemblance to actual persons living or dead, business establishments, events, or locales, is entirely coincidental.

You Can't Bury Death

COPYRIGHT © 2025 by Peggy Doviak

All rights reserved. No part of this book may be used or reproduced in any manner whatsoever including the purpose of training artificial intelligence technologies in accordance with Article 4(3) of the Digital Single Market Directive 2019/790, The Wild Rose Press expressly reserves this work from the text and data mining exception. Only brief quotations embodied in critical articles or reviews may be allowed. Contact Information: info@thewildrosepress.com

Cover Art by *Najla Mahis*

The Wild Rose Press, Inc.
PO Box 708
Adams Basin, NY 14410-0708
Visit us at www.thewildrosepress.com

Publishing History
First Edition, 2025
Trade Paperback ISBN 978-1-5092-6164-2
Digital ISBN 978-1-5092-6165-9

A Magnolia Hill Mystery
Published in the United States of America

Dedication

For my family, both by blood and by love.

Acknowledgments

I'm so excited for Jillian, Will, and Allie to solve another mystery! I've fallen in love with the characters, and I hope you have, too. I also hope my book has piqued your interest in the mounds at Spiro. Visit them if you are anywhere close because they are a unique look into First American Mississippian culture. A traveling exhibit of artifacts from the period occurred a few years ago, but nothing was stolen, and no one was murdered.

Thank you to my wonderful editor, Ally Robertson, for your overwhelming skill and support. Thank you, also, to my publisher, The Wild Rose Press, for taking such good care of me.

Huge thanks to Anna Vincent, the current Director of the Spiro Mounds Archeological Center, and Dennis Peterson, the former Director at Spiro. Your information about the history of the mounds was fascinating and helpful. Anything accurate is because of them, and all mistakes are mine.

Thank you to Chase Greeno, the Project Manager at the Fabrication Lab of the University of Oklahoma, for answering my questions about 3-D printing. The technology is incredible and improving every day.

Thank you to my publicist, Nancy Berland. You have been so helpful for so long. You've put me in the right places and introduced me to people I couldn't have met without you. I wouldn't have accomplished any of this if it weren't for you.

Thank you for all the support I receive from Writerspace, with extra love sent to Susan Simpson and warmest memories of Cissy Harley.

Thank you to my friends in the Tornado Alley

Chapter of Sisters in Crime for your support and encouragement. I'm lucky to have you in my life. Thanks, also, to my Route 66 Critique Group, also through Sisters in Crime, for your great ideas. Thank you to Jo Carol Jones for letting a personal finance author crash several author/reader events. Your support and networking have been so helpful, and I'm finally writing fiction! Thank you to all the amazing writer friends I met at Book Lovers Con. Thanks also to my Kauai retreat buddies. Your talent inspires me every day. Special thanks to Sheila Roberts for your support, friendship, and frequent conversations with your readers. You're awesome.

Thank you to my family, both by blood and by love. You all are the most important part of my life. Thank you to my friends, especially Jennene, Patty, and Marguerite, for listening to my ideas for longer than anyone should be required.

Finally, special thanks to my superfan, my aunt Margaret Beggs, who supports me in all ways possible, including feeding me! And forever thanks to my personal guardian angel, Richard Doviak.

Chapter One

"Mister, don't tear up that pumpkin," Jillian yelled. From the top of the ladder, she couldn't do anything else about his mischief without risking a broken leg or electrocution.

Mister, the black and white paint horse in the adjacent run, was worse than a vandalizing teen. He stared up at Jillian, gave a disgusted sigh, and backed up a step from the Halloween decorations on the posts of his run. Jillian's sorrel horse, Agatha, named for Agatha Christie, looked smugly at Mister and nodded her white-starred head up and down. Jillian laughed at her, and the behaving horse gazed up expectantly.

"Hang on, sweet girl, let me finish these lights and get off the ladder. Then, I'll give you a treat."

At the word "treat," Mister glanced up hopefully. "Yes, bad boy, you'll get one, too. I bet you're glad your mom lets me feed you." Jillian turned her attention back to the string of lights she was zip-tying to the barn wall in front of Agatha's run. Finally, after the last satisfying zip, she carefully climbed down the ladder. She pried open the metal trash can where she protected the treats from skunks, mice, and anything else wandering around during the night.

It was a week before Halloween, and financial planner Jillian Bradford was at Agatha's barn. Her happy place seemed a million emotional miles from cash flow statements and market returns. In addition to the newly strung smiling ghost lights, Jillian also attached solar-powered pumpkins to the metal posts of Agatha's run. Mister, who shared a line of fencing, thought they were a snack for him, but he hadn't appeared to do any damage.

Jillian leaned against the run's panels and turned around to admire her work. The white ghosts and orange pumpkins would brighten the gloom of night that came earlier these days. Agatha walked up behind Jillian and bumped her nose hard against her mom's arm. Jillian spun back around as the horse gave her a guilty look.

"No, ma'am. I know you want cookies, but don't be pushy." The red horse dropped her head and moved one foot backward. "That's more like it. Here are your treats." She fed the mare four peppermint nuggets, one at a time, and then walked over to Mister's run with four more. He gobbled them up while Agatha pinned her ears at them both.

All at once, Jillian and the two horses were startled by the sudden sound of calling birds. Jillian thought "calling" was too polite of a word. And they certainly weren't chirping. They were complaining, yelling, screaming. A massive cloud of grackles rose into the air from a distant pasture. Hundreds of birds flew in a black circle. Then, the circle stretched, dropped, and rose again, every bird somehow knowing how to move to stay in formation. From Agatha's run, they looked like smoke, making graceful curls over the pasture while expressing their anger about the impending winter.

Although their sound could be irritating, Jillian thought their formations were beautiful, and she enjoyed the scene momentarily. The Bermuda grass was beginning to lose its green with the reduced sunlight. Although the trees beyond the still ranch were primarily green, the yellows, oranges, and occasional reds were beginning to show. In the dimming light, scuddy clouds blocked both the setting sun and the rising moon. Although Jillian didn't need a jacket yet, the wind held the slightest risk of being cold. Far too soon, she'd be coming out to the barn in overalls and a hooded coat.

The horses didn't find the scene as compelling as Jillian did, and they soon turned back to her, hoping for another treat. "Okay, one more apiece, and then I've got to scoot. I need to run by my office and answer a client email before I can go home. I wish I had remembered my laptop, and I also wish she had written down her account number the last time I gave it to her." Jillian wore a smart watch to the barn to keep dust, hay, and who knows what from impacting her cell phone. Although she could read emails on the small screen, typing the answers was too tricky.

She turned to walk back to her truck, and her watch rang. Her dad's picture showed on the screen, and she answered happily. "Hi, Dad. Have you and Mom decided where you want to go to dinner tonight?"

Her ordinarily cheerful father sounded reserved. "Hi, Jilly. We don't want to disappoint you, but we need to cancel. Do you remember Fred Winkler, the director at the Spiro archeological site? We had a strange conversation today, and I'm going down there to meet with him."

Chapter Two

Jillian dropped her head at her father's words. "Oh, I'm sorry. I was looking forward to seeing you guys tonight." She loved spending time with her parents even though her father's archeology work often placed them in distant parts of the globe.

"We are, too. If we hadn't just returned from South America, we'd still have time to see you tonight, but we've got to do laundry and get organized. Fred sounded desperate to talk to me, and it's not like him to overreact. If he's worried, I need to go as soon as I can."

"I haven't seen him in ages," Jillian said. "He left the university several years ago to become the director at Spiro, didn't he?" She sat on a crunchy hay bale at the front of Agatha's run.

"Good memory," her father said with admiration. "You know he always loved the excavations, and when the directorship opened, he applied. He's lived down there for five years now."

"Oh, that's so cool. I've always loved Spiro." Jillian's visits to the archeological site spanned nearly her entire life. Less than 200 miles from Magnolia Hill, it contained the most extensive collection of Native American mounds west of the Mississippi. Until recently, it had been known as a trading center around 1000 AD, but new scholarship suggested that the site played a more critical role. Although it saw a lot of commerce because of nearby rivers, leading to a wide range of artifacts, Spiro also played an important religious part of the Mississippian culture.

Jillian remembered the fun she had as a child at the site. "Do you remember when you and Fred let me help you excavate?"

"Which time?" her father teased. "I think you're remembering the summer when we were sponsoring an undergraduate dig. You begged to come with me, and when we left, you were wearing khaki pants and a long-sleeved matching shirt."

"And by the time I'd been there thirty minutes, I went into the bathroom and changed into shorts and a tee shirt. I think I was ten, and I wanted to dress like the archeologists I saw in movies. But long sleeves don't work in the Oklahoma heat."

Her dad chuckled. "Fortunately, malaria isn't an issue in southeast Oklahoma. You were perfectly safe in your shorts."

Jillian pulled off her ball cap, smoothed her blonde hair, and pulled it back into a ponytail again, using the cap as the clip. "I think that was the trip where I found some beads and arrowheads."

"I remember. You were so proud of yourself. I thought you might choose archeology as a profession."

"I considered it, but I'm glad I chose a different path. I think I've landed where I'm supposed to be. I love helping people with their money. Besides, I can live vicariously through your adventures. What made Fred's call so strange?"

Jillian's dad paused before he answered. "He sounded upset, almost frightened. He told me he wanted to show me something at the site but didn't want to talk about it over the phone."

"What could possibly be going on at Spiro that he's concerned about?"

"I don't know unless it has something to do with the traveling Spiro artifact exhibit. I think I told you about it. A group of us have assembled artwork, weapons, and household items originally from the mounds. People from all over the world have lent pieces from their collections. It opened here on the fall solstice since Spiro is aligned with the seasons and then stays through Thanksgiving before it moves on to Dallas."

"That's so cool. Fred must be excited for the publicity the tour will bring to the site."

"He was enthusiastic before we left for Peru. I'm not sure what's happened in the last couple of weeks."

In spite of her jeans, the hay was beginning to poke Jillian. She raised herself and sat back down, buying herself a few more minutes of relief. "How were you able to leave for Peru in the middle of this?"

"I contacted the item's donors months ago. Fred and Don have done most of the hands-on work."

"Don White? You've worked with him at several sites, too, right?"

"I have. He's still at the university with me but loves Spiro as much as Fred and I do. I wonder if he knows why Fred is upset."

"I hope it isn't anything serious," Jillian said. "Are you driving down this evening?"

"No, he asked if I could stay a few days, so your mom and I need to finish the laundry, pack a couple of bags, and leave first thing in the morning. We'll be there before lunch."

"You're right. You've got too much work to have dinner tonight. You want me to bring you takeout?

"No, Jilly, we've stopped by the store earlier today. After three weeks of traveling in Peru, we want something simple like a sandwich. Even though I love lomo saltado and a pisco sour, a plain ham and cheese, ruffled potato chips, and a soda sound good tonight."

"Yum, I think putting meat and French fries into a single dish is one of the best ideas the Peruvians had. And I can't get a pisco sour anywhere, so I always settle for a margarita. I think I'm as jealous of the food you get to eat as much as the places you go. But I understand why you might be ready for a basic meal. Let me know when you get there tomorrow. You'll enjoy the fall foliage on the drive down. Southeast Oklahoma has some of the prettiest colored leaves in the state."

"That it does," her father agreed.

"And morning will be an easier drive," she continued. "I hate how early it gets dark this time of year. Tell Fred that I said hello. I want to go down and see the exhibition before it moves on."

"I will, sweetheart. We'll go to dinner as soon as we're back. Tell Will we'll see him then, too."

Jillian stood as she pressed the button on her watch face to disconnect the call. She brushed the hay off herself, thinking about how lucky she was. Her parents were supportive without prying. They knew if anything was wrong, she would tell them. She was sure they were happy about the positive changes in her relationship with Will Anderson, but they never made a big deal out of it.

She glanced around at Agatha's new Halloween decorations and saw her horse standing in the corner of her turnout, pawing with her front hoof. "Pretty girl, what are you doing?"

The horse gave her a baleful look and continued to scrape the ground. "Hey, stop that. You don't need to dig a hole." After a couple more scratches in the dirt, Agatha wandered back to Jillian for a final cookie. Jillian kissed her nose, fed her a snack, and gave one more to Mister. Now that her dinner plans had fallen through, she needed to figure out what she would eat after she found the information for her client.

Chapter Three

After finding the account information, Jillian left her office and drove home. She thought about the archeological digs she attended as a child with Fred, Don, and her dad. When she was too small to be trusted with a sift, they would call her over when they found something. She took still pictures and shot videos of them unearthing the artifacts. Jillian experienced the same excitement, whether it was an arrowhead or a ceremonial piece.

Her father was right about her interest in archeology, but as a freshman, she opted to major in English instead after a semester working on the college magazine. Then, when her grandmother fell victim to a stockbroker, she changed careers and went into finance. Now, she loved helping people understand their money.

Still, her life wasn't as glamorous as her father's Indiana Jones' lifestyle. Whenever she met someone who discovered what her father did for a living, they were always anxious to meet him and talk about the work that took him around the world. Any conversations she wanted to have about finances never held them spellbound like her dad's tales.

Her folks were gone last summer while she was trying to figure out how her ex-boyfriend, Stan Savage, was murdered. During that stressful time, her folks spent an extended period researching stone circles in England. At least her dad did. Her mom was more interested in making sure her father remembered to eat and didn't get himself into trouble. As an English major and writer, herself, she also published some fabulous travel blog posts.

Fred's wife and her mom were great friends, and she knew the foursome would have fun over the weekend, even if Fred was worried about something. Her dad and Fred were quite a pair. Fred was a saint for answering Jillian's endless questions. He was also quirky, and his hair blew everywhere, like Einstein's.

Jillian's journey into the past ended when she turned into the driveway of her home. She opened the door and slipped off her barn boots as her black cat Edgar, named for Edgar Allan Poe, wove around her ankles, begging for pets and something to eat. She picked him up and carried him to the kitchen, where she kissed his head and deposited him on the floor again. "Did you miss me, boy?"

Edgar chirped as she reached for a can of his food, and he was soon happily gobbling away. Jillian knew she must be hungry if she was jealous of his shredded tuna substance. She needed to eat, so she texted Will and asked if he wanted to grab a bite.

Will Anderson was a reporter for the *Magnolia Daily*. A long-ago misunderstanding kept them from speaking for years, no small accomplishment given the population of Magnolia Hill. However, Will had proven himself to be a good friend over the summer, and eventually, he explained his actions from all those years ago. Shortly after the 4th of July, Jillian and Will started dating, and even though the relationship was new, Jillian was happy and excited about their future together.

When her phone rang, Will's picture came up on her caller ID. It was a casual shot she had captured late in the summer, but she thought it nicely highlighted his dark, curly hair and green eyes. Jillian's heart beat faster.

"Hi, Jilly. I hate to say this, but I won't be able to eat dinner with you and your folks tonight. I got a call from Amber, and she's worried about something. She's coming by the paper later and wants to ask me some questions."

"Shoot. That's the third time this week that something's come up. You need to help Amber?" Jillian hoped her disappointment and mild irritation didn't carry to the emphasis she placed on the name. Will's sigh let her know the sharpness was apparent.

"Yes, Amber. You know, she's moved back to Magnolia Hill."

"No, I didn't." Jillian knew Will and Amber had dated years ago. Although back in July, Jillian encouraged Will to reach out to Amber and clear the air over a long-gone misunderstanding, she wasn't thrilled that his ex-girlfriend moved back to town.

"What was I supposed to do?" Will sounded frustrated. "She asked me for my help. I don't know why."

Jillian took a deep breath. "Would you like for me to bring you a sandwich?" she managed to ask kindly.

Will paused. "Amber told me she'd bring dinner to the office. I'm sorry. She said it's important. I thought it would be okay since you could still eat with your folks. You haven't had much time to see them since they got home."

"So you thought you'd have dinner with Amber

instead of us? Fine. Have a nice evening." Jillian heard Will say something as she hung up the phone. Almost immediately, he rang back, but she didn't want to talk to him. She'd eat dinner by herself, then. She didn't need anyone else to have a good meal. Edgar hopped up beside her. At least she still had her cat. She petted him on his head, and he closed his eyes and purred.

Chapter Four

Jillian ignored a second call from Will and a text asking her to call him. Instead, she checked the time. Maybe Allie would like to get a quick cup of coffee and later dinner.

Allie Kowalski was Jillian's best friend since grade school. Allie was a visual artist, a painter, who paid her bills by also painting practical items like doors, fences, and walls for grateful clients. Additionally, she did commissions and custom work and had recently finished a beautiful crib adorned with a baby girl mermaid painted in pinks and turquoises.

Allie's appearance gave tribute to her Polish heritage. She had expressive, blue eyes and a pale blonde, short bob cut. Sometimes, she added intentional stripes of color to her hair, and she always had unintentional paint somewhere on her face, arms, or clothes.

After a few minutes, Allie texted back. She would love to grab a coffee but already made dinner plans with her boyfriend, Ace.

Jillian shot back a smiley face and a single word, — *Kandace's?*—

When she got a thumbs up, she took down her ponytail and brushed out her shoulder-length blonde hair. She had cut off a few inches in September and liked the results. It was professional while still giving her the convenience of being able to pull it back or up. She quickly changed into wide-leg jeans, an orange sweater, and black loafers. After a scary incident over the summer, she checked that her house was locked before she jumped into her pickup and headed to town.

Allie's tangerine Prius was already parked in front of Bits, Bytes, and Brews when Jillian pulled in beside her. Somehow, Allie always managed to arrive first. Once inside, Jillian glanced around the chrome and tile internet cafe until she spotted Allie's light blonde hair in the corner. As she approached the table, she saw orange flecks splattered all over Allie's green and black plaid shirt and distressed jeans. Her hair even shimmered with orange glitter. Allie shot her a huge grin.

"Hey, Jillian, great idea! I needed a break."

"What have you been working on?" Jillian asked, hiding her amusement.

"I've been using a toothbrush to cover pumpkins in orange glitter."

"That explains why you sparkle."

Allie shrugged. "It might be my personality. Seriously, I don't think I own any clothes that don't have paint on them somewhere. Paint, glitter, stain, you name it."

"What's it for?"

"Magnolia Hill's Arts Council is decorating Loving Care nursing home for Halloween. I volunteered to help with the foam pumpkins. I love seeing the residents' faces when we set everything up."

"That's so cool. Good for you."

Before Jillian could say anything further, Kandace O'Connor, the owner of the coffee shop and internet cafe, rolled up in her electric wheelchair. "Hey, friends," she said cheerfully. "What can I get you?"

"Anything pumpkin spiced?" Allie asked hopefully.

"You know it. I can do a pumpkin chai latte. I know you're a chai fan," Kandace said. "What about you, Jilly?"

"I'll have a pumpkin-spiced latte. I'm so glad it's finally pumpkin season again."

"We're going all out this year. Stop in often," Kandace offered.

"You know you don't have to invite us twice," Jillian said.

"You won't want to miss our baked goods. We're offering pumpkin pecan squares, pumpkin muffins, and pumpkin cream rolls."

"Yum," Allie and Jillian said together.

The jingling bell on the door announcing new customers interrupted their conversation. Officer Gayle Johnson walked into the shop talking to another officer Jillian didn't know. She whispered over to Kandace. "Who's beside Gayle, and where's Jeff?"

Jillian had known Gayle since high school and believed she stood for everything good about the police department. Her partner, Jeff Stone, didn't impress her as much. Over the summer, he had resented her participation in a case, even though she had eventually helped solve it.

"Didn't you hear?" Allie murmured. "Jeff retired last month."

"Good for him," Jillian said. "Even though he wasn't my favorite person, he deserves to relax. Being a police officer would be stressful. Who's the new guy?"

"His name is Bud Bowden," Kandace volunteered.

"He's from Big Sky, and he's Gayle's new partner."

Jillian was committed to Will, but she still appreciated the new officer's muscular physique, short blond hair, and blue eyes. Or were they green? She couldn't tell from where she was sitting.

"Lucky Gayle," she laughed, and Allie and Kandace joined in. Hearing her name, Gayle looked over at the table and waved at them before she and Bud stood at the counter to place their order.

"I've met him a few times," Kandace said. "He's as nice as he is cute, and I don't think he has a girlfriend."

"You could help him with that," Jillian said to Kandace, and her friend blushed.

"I think I should focus on your order, instead." Kandace rolled back until she could see behind the counter. "Lucas, can you get me a pumpkin chai latte and a pumpkin spiced latte?"

"No problem." The older teen grinned. Jillian marveled at his transformation. More than three months ago, Kandace gave Lucas a second chance, and the teen grabbed hold of it with both hands. Now, he worked tirelessly in the shop and even ran personal errands for Kandace if she needed them.

Kandace saw Jillian watching Lucas. "Remarkable, isn't it?"

Jillian nodded. She had been skeptical, but Lucas proved her wrong.

"I'm glad I took a chance on him," Kandace continued. "I don't think anyone ever believed in him before, and now I don't know how I ran the place without him."

Kandace was mostly wheelchair-bound since a hit-and-run accident in high school, but the tragedy hadn't slowed her down. Her ability to create a successful coffee shop and internet cafe surprised no one. Kandace appeared tireless, but Jillian was sure she appreciated not having to do everything herself.

After the beverages arrived, Kandace rolled away to greet other patrons, and Jillian summarized Amber's focus on Will to Allie. The orange speckles on her cheeks bobbed left and right as she shook her head in irritation.

"Well, broomsticks! I wonder what Amber's up to," she finally said. "I hope she isn't making a play for Will. But you know it won't work. Will's crazy about you."

Jillian knew her friend was supportive, so she didn't dare laugh. Allie's grandmother, Penny Kroll, hated profanity. As a result, Allie developed unique and successful ways of expressing emotions. And Penny was such a wonderful person, both as a grandmother and as a friend, that Jillian and Allie respected her wishes.

"Well, I hope so," Jillian said, "but I don't like the fact that Will won't tell me what's going on."

Allie chuckled. "You guys do need to work on your communication skills. Still, I don't think it's anything. You're sure he's keeping a secret?"

"He did try to call me a couple of times after I hung up on him," Jillian admitted, lowering her gaze.

"Jumping zombies," Allie exclaimed. "And you're mad that he won't talk to you?"

Jillian relented. "Okay, I'll give him a call. You don't want to get a snack?" she asked sadly.

"I've already promised Ace we'd get a pizza, and then, those pumpkins won't glitter themselves. I have to be finished tomorrow, so I'm going to stay up late tonight. Rain check?"

"Of course." Jillian finished her latte, noticing Allie's cup was already empty. "I'll let you go. Call me after you get up tomorrow." With a wave to Kandace and Lucas, she left the cheery room, got in her truck, and drove home.

Chapter Five

Jillian picked up a takeout burger and fries from her favorite fast-food restaurant. She judged burger joints by their French fries more than their sandwiches, and as far as she was concerned, this place was the best and close enough to her home that the food would stay hot.

As she opened her front door, Edgar trotted out to see her. He rubbed his head against her jeans, and his back legs stretched out one at a time.

"Hi, kitty. Did you miss me?"

Edgar offered a cheerful meow in reply. Since the day she found the black kitten with giant green eyes at the barn, Edgar had been affectionate. After asking around, she decided he had likely been dropped by someone who thought he could live by eating mice at the stables. At that point, he was only the size of about three mice, himself. She figured he was more likely to become a coyote's breakfast, so she brought him home. Edgar quickly learned that beds, couches, and cat food were far better than roaming around on a scary night.

Now, he followed her to the kitchen. She got out a red Fiestaware plate, opened the burger box, and poured the fries in the other half of the box to keep them off the cold pottery. She grabbed a bottle of soda from the fridge and sat down at her wooden kitchen table. She slipped off her loafers and stretched out her legs across the

Navajo cushions of the chair beside her.

As she munched away at her burger, she also ate the fries three at a time, trying to finish them while they were still hot. Edgar sat on her lap, begging for little bites of hamburger meat. She knew fast food wasn't good for him, but he was so cute. Besides, she justified, it was only a small amount, and he wasn't overweight.

She knew Allie was right about not staying angry with Will, so she texted him. —*Busy?*— She waited for his response, but nothing popped up on her screen. Her heart dropped.

Why was she always so suspicious? She reminded herself that some people deserved her doubt, like her ex-boyfriend, Stan. Her distrust of him was more than justified. But many people, including Will, were kind and at least relatively honest.

Still, she wished Will would have kept her in the loop about Amber. Why was she being secretive about what she wanted Will to do? She briefly wondered if Amber was telling Will the truth, and then she sighed. She was being suspicious again. She was sure she'd hear from Will soon, and when she did, she'd try to explain how important it was to her that they talk about things with each other.

She set her dishes on the counter and then washed them by hand, an easy task since most of the crumbs landed in the cardboard box. Fiestaware chipped, so she hated to put it in the dishwasher.

Disgusted with Will and herself, Jillian plopped down on her brown leather couch and clicked the remote. A reality show was ending, and the news would start soon. She checked some social media on her phone while she waited for the latest relationship story to end.

She glanced up once to see a bikini-clad brunette sobbing into the camera while the split screen showed a blonde kissing a well-chiseled guy. How could people watch that stuff? Did they believe any of it? Relationships were complicated, and she couldn't imagine playing out a fight with Will while television cameras rolled. She started to read her phone again when the evening news began with grainy, nighttime footage of half a dozen blue lights, like lanterns, bobbing over the top of a hill. The lights rose and fell, too dim to cast a shadow. The chyron under the image read, "Has the ghost returned to Spiro?"

Jillian grabbed the remote and raised the volume. The off-screen reporter spoke in ominous tones. "This video was captured last night by some teens who entered the park after it was closed. They claimed to be halfway between Craig Mound and Brown Mound. The teens admitted to drinking beer, but their video evidence confirms what others have been suggesting. Are the spirits active at Spiro mounds again?"

Chapter Six

Jillian knew her mom and dad always stayed up later than ten o'clock. As soon as the story ended, she called her father. "By any chance, are you watching the news?"

"We were. This certainly puts a new spin on things."

"Do you think the story has broken in Spiro yet? I bet this is what has Fred so upset."

"You know, if it's news in Oklahoma City, it's bigger news in Fort Smith, and I'm sure it's already on the networks there. Anyway, I'll find out from Fred soon enough. Your mom and I are driving down there right after breakfast."

"Be safe. The weather is good tomorrow, so that will make it easy. And I envy you seeing the foliage. Now, I might be jealous that you could see a ghost."

"I don't know about that, but it should be pretty. I'm afraid the last of it will be slow, though. I was checking my phone's map before you called, and I watched the traffic color change from yellow to orange. Seems like all the looky-loos want to see a ghost. The backed-up cars start from the north of Spiro at Sallisaw and the east at Fort Smith. The traffic is worst in Spiro, and you know it never has a traffic jam."

"I can't imagine Fred truly angry, but I bet he's irritated," Jillian said. "If you see any blue lights, let me know. It would be fun to drive down for the weekend and experience some ghostly spirits. Love you and Mom."

Her dad laughed. "You'll be my first call. Talk to you later. Love you more."

The next morning, Jillian thought about the Spiro news report as she dressed in work clothes—a white long-sleeved shirt and black slacks. She slipped on black heels and finished the outfit with black jewelry. She pulled her hair in a messy bun, applied light makeup, and spritzed on cologne. She would like to see the blue lights if they were real, and that was a big if. Likely, someone was pulling a prank a few days before Halloween. The evening news probably filled some extra time with a local ghost story. But still, it would be an adventure. On a whim, she pulled out her cell phone to call Allie. If Will wanted to spend time with Amber, she'd give him the weekend to do it.

When her friend answered the phone, Jillian jumped right to the point. "Did you see the news last night?"

"I saw the beginning, but then I went back to work on my pumpkin project. Ace and I spent too long at dinner, so I was up late."

"There are worse problems to have," Jillian offered.

"Isn't that the truth," Allie agreed. "We had a great time, but I had to finish the glittering, so I could drop them off at the nursing home this morning."

"Does that mean you're free this weekend?"

"As soon as I get them delivered. Why?"

"Wanna go on a ghost hunt?"

"What? Do you mean the lights down at Spiro? I saw the story right before I started working again."

"Yeah, I talked to Dad. We both think that's why Fred asked him if he could come. He and Mom had no idea what was going on until they saw the news report."

"So, do the people in Spiro believe the ghosts are back?"

"Maybe. I don't know. I thought I might drive down there for the weekend and check it out. I wondered if you wanted to come."

"I'm surprised you didn't call Will. Have you not talked to him yet?" Allie's concern sounded in her voice.

"I tried, but he didn't answer. I'll try again this morning. I promise. I'll tell him you and I are going down to help Dad."

"I'm in. What time do you want to pick me up?"

"Maybe about 1:00. I'd like to get there before it's dark, but I've got a client meeting this morning. And I should call first to make sure we can get a room. Dad said the city seems to have a traffic jam."

"I'll be ready at 1:00, but I'll only leave if you promise me you've talked to Will."

Chapter Seven

Jillian pulled her truck in front of her office located in the historic downtown section of Magnolia Hill. Her floor-to-ceiling windows looked out on what could be a set for a Western movie. An antique hitching post was preserved on the sidewalk, but these days, residents attached bicycles instead of horses. People would think she was crazy if she rode Agatha to the office and left her there until she was finished with her day. She smiled at the image as she prepared for a new client meeting.

Her assistant Katherine had a dental appointment, and even though she had prepared most of the paperwork in advance, Jillian always liked to review everything. Her new prospect, Ben Lurch, had left a phone message asking to talk to her, but he hadn't provided any other details. After she was prepared, she checked her watch but didn't have enough time to call Will.

Ben Lurch arrived about an hour after she did, and his tall, pale appearance made Jillian's spine chill. Only around Halloween would Jillian meet a new client named Lurch, who appeared to be more like a specter than a mortal. When she asked Ben how she could help him, she swallowed hard as he began to speak in a faint voice with over-pronounced ss's that made him sound like he was hissing.

"I appressiate your answswering my messsage sso

ssoon," he said earnestly, gazing directly at her with pale blue, watery eyes.

She avoided meeting his gaze. "I'm happy to do it, Mr. Lurch. Now, what would you like to talk to me about?"

"SSince Patssy, my late wife, passsed, I've dessided that I want to create a trusst to keep my kidss from sspending my money too fasst. I might be deceassed, but that won't sstop me."

Maybe it was his weird vocal patterns, but Jillian rested her arms on the conference table to keep herself from trembling. This dude was frightening.

"Mr. Lurch, I'd love to help you, but I'm not an attorney. I know that you can have a lawyer create a document, likely a trust, that will help you meet your goals. But I'm not the right person to assist you. I'm a financial planner, not an attorney, and I can't cross the line into giving legal advice."

"I ssee," he hissed. "Pleasse recommend ssomeone." He rubbed his hands together like he was washing them. Or, perhaps, he was viewing her recommendation as a delicious snack.

Jillian briefly weighed her options. She liked the people she referred, and Mr. Lurch was creepy. Of course, the firm could opt not to take him as a client. She gave the man a local attorney's card, shook his cold hand, and wished him a nice day. As soon as he was outside, she went into the bathroom and washed her still-clammy hand with soap and water. Then, she called the attorney she recommended. She didn't give her the name of the potential client, but she summarized her referral.

Her friend choked on the other end of the phone. "So, you've sent me a ghoul for a client? Thanks a lot."

"He's not a real monster. I think. But he's creepy as the dickens. I hope he pays you well." She laughed as she hung up the phone and turned her attention back to the blue lights. She texted Katherine and let her dedicated employee know that Mr. Lurch hadn't worked out and would not be a client. She'd fill her in on the details in person. Then, she turned off her laptop and headed home.

Jillian quickly changed clothes to stretchy jean leggings and a long-sleeved T-shirt. She packed a few things in a gym bag and called Allie. "I got done early. The last client wasn't a good fit for our firm. Could we leave sooner than one o'clock?"

"Sure," Allie agreed. "I dropped off the pumpkins at 9:00, took an extra shower to help with the glitter, and now, I'm ready whenever you are."

"Great, I'll pick you up in half an hour."

Edgar narrowed his green eyes at Jillian indignantly and offered a loud, angry meow.

"Don't worry, buddy. I'll be back in a couple days. I'll leave you multiple bowls of food, water, and an extra litter box. You'll be fine."

She swore she heard him huff as he turned from her and walked away. She watched him until she saw him jump on her bed. Then, she grabbed her bag and headed for the truck. She thought about wearing her barn work boots, but she wanted something cleaner, so at the last minute, she grabbed some hiking boots that she kept for the rare occasions when she walked outdoors.

As she approached Allie's condo decorated with Talavera pottery and flower baskets now rangy from the shorter days, her friend opened her door, grabbed a duffel bag, and bounded into the truck. "I know there will be a logical explanation for all of this, but I hope we get to see the blue lights."

"Me, too," Jillian agreed. "Want to grab a quick cheeseburger at Donny's Drive-In?"

When Allie nodded, Jillian turned her truck onto a major street running through Magnolia Hill, and soon, they were ordering cheeseburgers and onion rings along with a pumpkin-spiced latte for Jillian and a soda for Allie.

"I don't know how you drink hot beverages with hamburgers," Allie said. "I need something cold. Burgers weren't designed for coffee."

"Everything's designed for coffee," Jillian disagreed. The carhop on roller skates soon appeared with their food, and when Jillian opened the bag, the heavenly scent of onion rings filled her cab. The cornmeal-breaded sweet onions weren't quite as good as those from Burger Bonanza, but they were a close second. Their conversation ceased as they devoured the meals.

"Man, that was yummy." Jillian wiped up her catsup with the last onion ring. She bagged their trash and wadded it into a ball then tossed the bag into an open waste can and turned onto the road. "We've saved time, so we'll get there early."

Once she was on the state highway that led directly into Spiro, she glanced over at Allie. "Tell me how things are with you and Ace."

Allie's fair skin blushed bright pink. "We're good, really good. I think we've both grown up since high school, and we're more confident talking about what we want in the future."

"Any news I need to know?" Jillian asked with

surprise.

"Not yet. I would tell you," Allie promised. "Right now, we're happy to be getting reacquainted. I can't imagine losing him again from my life, but we don't want to rush into anything." Allie and Ace dated in high school, and back then, Ace wanted to get married, but Allie wanted to go to college first. Their different goals drew them apart.

Jillian was glad to see them back together even though she supported her friend's earlier decision. "I'm so happy for both of you. You guys always brought out the best in each other."

"That we do," Allie agreed. "I do have news that I've intended to share with you, but it's not about me."

"So it's not news, it's gossip?"

"Gossip, shmossip," Allie opened both of her hands palms up and shrugged.

"So, spill the tea."

"You saw Gayle's new partner, Bud, yesterday at Kandace's."

"I did," Jillian agreed as she turned the truck onto the state highway. She thought it might get her to Spiro more directly than taking the interstate even though the speed limit wasn't as fast.

"Did you hear Kandace say that Bud was nice?"

"Yes, and then I teased her, and she changed the subject."

"She changed the subject because, according to Gayle, Kandace and Bud have had dinner twice."

"Really?" Jillian exclaimed. "I love that."

"Gayle does, too," Allie agreed. "She thinks Bud really likes Kandace, and judging by Kandace's response, I think the feeling might be mutual. They don't want to talk about it until they give it some more time, so please don't say anything."

"I won't. Kandace deserves someone who sees her for the incredible person she is."

"Apparently, it started when Kandace special ordered some coffee beans for Bud. Yes, she does it for any customer who requests it, but Bud was impressed. He's gone into the shop often in his short time here."

"Kandace always tries to make her patrons feel special. Apparently, this time, she really succeeded," Jillian laughed.

"Right. Bud and Gayle have hours to talk. Apparently, Bud has a mother who uses an electric scooter part of the time. She has a form of arthritis. Bud's been around adaptive equipment most of his life, and he doesn't think it's a big deal."

"That's the best news I've heard in a long time. Good for him. Now, I hope they really like each other. Relationships are so complicated."

"That they are," Allie agreed. "Speaking of that, did you ever bother to call Will?"

Jillian focused on the road, and Allie cleared her throat. "Have you talked to Will?"

"Not yet. I tried," she justified. "I promise I'll call him again once we get settled at the motel."

"I don't want you to screw this up because you've assumed the wrong things."

"I don't either." Jillian sighed. "I was thinking earlier that I shouldn't be so suspicious. I know it's wrong. I'll give him a call as soon as we get there."

"Do it now," Allie insisted.

"Okay." Jillian used her hands-free system to call Will. He picked up on the second ring.

"Jilly, you've been ignoring me."

Even though she was looking out the window, Allie shook her head and mumbled something under her breath.

"I'm sorry. I shouldn't have gotten upset."

"Why are you mad?" he asked sadly. Jillian's heart broke as she realized the power of her words.

Allie spoke up. "Hi, Will. I wanted to let you know I'm here, too."

"Hi, Allie. Where are you guys? We'll talk about Amber in a second."

"We're driving to Spiro," Jillian said. "My dad's already down here with my mom."

A long pause on the other end of the phone was followed by Will's laugh. "Are you girls chasing ghosts?"

"Careful, Will," Allie warned. "You're already in trouble."

Will chuckled harder. "I know. I'm making my situation worse, aren't I?"

"Uh huh," Allie agreed.

In spite of herself, Jillian also smiled. "Yes, Will, we're going on a ghost hunt in Spiro."

"Well, now I'm upset that I made y'all mad. I wish I could have come with you."

"I'm sure you don't want to share a room with both of us, and my dad pulled huge strings to get us one room in the motel where he's staying. Apparently, as soon as the story aired last night, everyone and their dog wanted to visit Spiro. You know there aren't many local motels, although I guess people could stay in Sallisaw or Fort Smith."

"I'm still sorry I'm missing it. Didn't you used to go

there with your dad when you were little?"

"I did. Since it's an important site and relatively close to Magnolia Hill, Dad and his colleagues, Don White and Fred Winkler, came down to the site often, especially in the summer. They let me take pictures of the artifacts they found, and eventually, they let me help them dig. I think the attention to detail I learned as I sifted dirt has helped me a lot as an adult."

"I'm sure it has," Will agreed. "I hope you guys see something cool. Hey, back to why I wasn't invited." He paused, and Jillian knew that although he used light words, he wasn't kidding. "Can you just trust me about Amber right now? I promise I'll explain it as soon as I can."

Allie vigorously nodded her head, her short blonde hair bobbing up and down. Jillian smiled at her friend's loyalty to the people she liked. "I can," she answered. "I trust you. Really, I do. But I don't understand why you can't tell me about it."

"Because I promised her I wouldn't. But as soon as she gives me the go-ahead, you'll be the first person I talk to. Honest. Allie, you can be the second."

Allie grinned, and her smile showed in her voice. "It's okay, Will, I'm on your side."

"Glad to hear it. Put in a good word for me from time to time, will you?" Will asked.

"I've got your back," Allie promised. "I do it all the time. Hey, back to what you were telling me about your dad. I know Don White."

"How? I thought he was retired." Jillian believed Don must be in his seventies since he was older than her father.

"Nope. Not completely. He told me he's only

teaching one class at a time now, and he has a teaching assistant to help with that."

"Sounds like a cushy job. But you can't know him through the Archeology Department."

"No, through the gallery where I show. Even though he's a super talented painter, he still takes classes."

"That doesn't surprise me. I suspect he enjoys learning new things."

"He's a great guy. He reminds me of Norman Rockwell with his palette. You know the painting I'm talking about?" Jillian nodded. Rockwell's self-portrait was iconic.

"Yes, I can see that. I wonder if Fred called him, too. I'm sure he's heard about the blue lights by now. Fred was always more fun than Don, but Don was remarkably tolerant of my participation. I need to ask my dad if he's talked to him recently."

Jillian glanced in her rearview mirror and saw the blazing sun lowering in the autumn sky. The orange and red light enhanced the colors of the leaves that were beginning to turn. Most fall foliage in the state was yellow and orange, but the wild sumac was a glorious red. Southeast Oklahoma was hillier and more wooded than the land around Magnolia Hill, and Jillian took a deep breath, feeling like she was returning to a place that always made her happy.

"I'm glad we left when we did. We'll be to Spiro before dark. With cars flying across the highway without traffic lights, Highway 9 isn't always fun when I can't see."

"Be careful," Will whispered. "I do care about you."

"I know you do," Jillian said, her voice catching. "I care about you, too. I'll keep you updated on our adventure."

She ended the call and glanced again at the map. They were only about ten miles from the motel.

As she pulled into the parking lot, she was surprised to see her father standing outside the motel's lobby under a neon sign that belonged to a time decades in the past. Jillian wondered if the turquoise doors on the rooms and midcentury modern lines were retro, or was the place actually that old? She suspected the latter.

She pulled into a parking place with faded lines, jumped out of her truck, and started to give her dad a hug. He reached for her absently, and she saw worry lines around his eyes. She looked around quickly for her mother and saw her standing in front of a guest room, clutching a tissue tightly in her hands. Had she been crying?

"Mom, Dad, what's wrong?"

Chapter Eight

Jillian's dad put his arm around her. "We'll talk about it in a minute. Let's get you checked in first."

The motel lobby confirmed Jillian's belief that it was old, not retro. White vinyl tile covered the floor, and the walls were painted in chipped turquoise. A tube television sat behind the check-in counter, and was obviously for the enjoyment of the employees, not the motel guests. In one corner, an ancient soda machine announced that it was out of most types of beverages. Beside it, a silver ice machine chugged, occasionally shooting out a cube that clattered against its walls. Allie walked up to the counter, prepared to pay for her half of the motel room, but Jillian's father shook his head no. He pulled out his credit card and tried to hand it to the clerk.

The curly-headed woman was focused on the television and didn't notice him at first. Jillian glanced to see what captured the young woman's attention. She was disappointed that the girl was watching a game show rerun that might be as old as the building. Too bad. Jillian was hoping she was distracted by a story about blue flames.

She started to ask the clerk if she knew anything about the ghost, but she glanced back at her mom and dad, who were obviously concerned about something. She'd talk to the clerk later.

"Dad, you don't need to pay for our room," she protested.

"Here, let me give you some cash," continued Allie, but he shook his head again.

"No need, girls. I know you wouldn't have come down if I weren't here. I'm sure you had other plans for the weekend."

Jillian and Allie burst out laughing. "No," Jillian said. "Ghost hunting is a bit of a treat." Her dad's lips drew tighter, stopping her. "Let's get our stuff out of the truck, and then you can tell us what's wrong."

The four of them walked over to the room, and Allie unlocked the door and turned the handle. As Jillian stepped inside, a faint hint of cigarette smoke washed over her. When was the last time it was legal to smoke in hotel rooms? As she looked around the retro bedroom, she figured the olive-green chintz bedspread, along with space-age, plastic olive-green chairs and a white Formica table, might have been purchased about the same time.

Jillian's dad saw her curled nose. "Sorry. Ours looks and smells the same. I wanted to get something closer than Fort Smith. Many of the places were already full. I was lucky to find something with two rooms."

"I bet everything filled up once the news of the blue flames broke," Jillian said. "Have you talked to Fred?"

Jillian's mom caught her breath, and her dad stared down at his hands before he glanced up. "Sort of." Jillian looked at them, confused, and her father continued. "We got here a little before noon, and I called Fred. He told me he was anxious to share something with me, and I offered to drive to the park, so we could talk." Her dad slumped on the side of the soft bed where he was sitting. "I wish I'd driven straight there, but he told me not to.

He was insistent he wanted to talk to me away from the park. I told him I needed to attend a short ZOOM meeting at 1:00 and offered to meet him here at 1:30. He promised to come, but he never arrived."

Allie's huge blue eyes grew even larger, and she stared at Jillian's father. "Ghosts and goblins. What do you mean he never arrived?"

"He never got here. I've called and called, but his phone goes straight to voicemail. I drove to the park, and his car's in the lot. What's weird is the guards said he told them goodbye around noon."

"Why are there guards?" Allie asked.

"The Visitor's Center needed additional security for the Spiro artifact exhibit. I don't know if Jillian told you that back in the thirties, most of Spiro's excavated items were sold off. Now, you can find the artifacts in museums and private collections all over the world, even the Louvre and the British Museum."

"Wow," Allie said. "I didn't know that."

Jillian's father continued. "The collected exhibit started here, but the Center's regular security didn't need to be as vigorous as now. Outside guards have been hired to keep the collection safe. It's irreplaceable."

"And the guards didn't see anything else unusual?" Jillian asked.

"No, other than huge crowds of tourists, who are sadly interested in ghosts, not history. I'm sure Fred wanted to talk to me about the exhibit or the news about the lights, but I can't imagine where he's gone."

"Is there any chance he wasn't feeling good, and his wife picked him up?" Allie asked.

"No, I called Suzanne. Fred was excited we were coming down here. He told her he wanted to talk to me, but she didn't know why. He left for work this morning and never came back."

"Don't panic," Jillian said, laying her hand on her dad's arm. He and her mom acted as young as Jillian's friends, but stress tightened their faces and aged them past their sixty-something years. Now, her dad appeared frail. "I'm sure there's a logical explanation. Do you have plenty of charge on your phone?" He nodded. "Do you have any signal?" she continued.

"Remarkably, I have plenty of signal. That's a major technology improvement in this part of the state. Cell service and wi-fi are critical for research."

"Then don't worry. I'm sure something came up, and he'll call."

"But he doesn't have his car."

"I know, but I don't have any idea what else you can do. I'm pretty sure the police won't do much yet. It's only been about six hours since you talked to him. If you haven't heard by tomorrow morning, give them a call. They might be able to issue a BOLO."

"Good idea. Having others on the lookout for him would help," her dad said. "Don's fine. He has to be. Let's get you both settled. Do you want to unpack or go grab a bite of dinner?"

"Grab a bite of dinner," Jillian and Allie exclaimed together.

"After that, I'd like to drive by the park," Jillian said. "I know it won't be open, but maybe we can see something if we get close to the bridge."

"Maybe," her dad said. "But I suspect no one is trying to keep people out of the park tonight. Honestly, the publicity is good for the site and the exhibit. With the traffic jam your mom and I saw coming in, the problem might be the park being big enough to hold all the people. Come on. There's a diner next door. You should hunt for ghosts on a full stomach."

Chapter Nine

The diner offered a chicken fried special that night. Patrons could order chicken fried chicken or chicken fried steak for discounted prices. Everyone opted for the steak. Jillian always thought it was funny that chicken fried steak was neither chicken nor traditional steak. Instead, cube steak was pounded thin, battered, and fried. Jillian ordered it with traditional sides of gravy, mashed potatoes with more gravy, green beans, and a soft roll. She ate every bite, and then waddled out of the diner. She and Allie hugged her mom and dad and told them not to wait up. Then, they drove a short distance down Highway 9 and headed north toward the park. Immediately, they were in bumper-to-bumper traffic.

"Ghostbusters. Is there another way?" asked Allie.

"Not easily," Jillian admitted. "But don't worry. It's not a long distance." Still, it took them almost an hour to drive the few miles, and when they got there, Jillian parked her truck on the side of the street. She didn't even bother to try to find a place in the small parking lot.

In spite of her concern for her folks and Fred, she was excited. She bounded out the door and called out a cheery, "Let's go find a ghost," when she noticed Allie was still sitting in the truck. Her sneakers were drawn up on the seat, and her arms were wrapped around her knees.

"What's wrong?"

"I have a bad feeling about all of this. I've changed my mind. I don't think I want to see a ghost. I don't like things I don't understand."

Jillian stopped for a minute, considering Allie's words. "You don't have to come if you don't want," she said. "You can stay in the truck."

"By myself?" Allie yelped.

"Well, yeah. I want to go check it out."

"Wait for me, then. Sitting alone in the dark is scarier than walking through a dark, haunted park with you. I think."

"I agree. And, besides, look around. We're anything but alone." Jillian gestured to the bobbing lights all over the park. "Those lights aren't blue, and they aren't created by ghosts. They're ghost hunters or normal people. Like us." Allie nodded and climbed out of the truck.

Jillian continued. "I don't think the ghosts are back. I'm sure people are experiencing some kind of elaborate prank. Why would the ghosts be back? No one is disturbing the artifacts."

"I don't know," Allie disagreed. "Remember, all the artifacts are gathered for the exhibit. Maybe together, they have triggered some kind of cosmic energy."

"Maybe. Let's go find out." She practically dragged Allie down the path toward the small bridge that separated the site from the Visitor's Center and parking lot. Crunchy leaves had begun to fall. As they broke into little pieces under Jillian's feet, they released a pungent odor that reminded her of being young and jumping into leaves that she and Allie carefully raked in the backyard. The piles weren't huge because they didn't have a lot of trees. Still, they were great memories.

As they approached the site, trees lined the creek, hanging onto their dying leaves with all their might. It was impossible to see anything except filtered light that moved with the wind. When they crossed the bridge into the open field, a waxing moon danced through thin clouds and provided remarkable light. To their right, imposing Craig Mound rose out of the shadows. It was the main location of the more impressive artifacts looted in the thirties. It was an unusual structure in that bodies were buried in its sides, but the center was open and originally filled with treasure. Through time, most people who reported seeing the blue lights reported them around Craig Mound. Tonight, Craig was covered and surrounded by lights, but none of them appeared to be ghostly. Most explorers stayed on the path around its base, either shining lights toward the mound to illuminate it or at each other to scare or tease friends. One couple even carried flashlights covered in blue plastic wrap. Jillian pointed them out to Allie.

"Look, Allie, blue lights," she snickered.

Allie glared at her. "You know, if there really are spirits out here, those fools are making them angry."

Jillian grabbed her friend's hand. "Oh, come on. It's just a little Halloween fun. Follow me. I've got a better plan."

Instead of turning right toward Craig and joining the multitude of bobbing lights, Jillian headed left down an asphalt path.

"Where are we going?" Allie asked.

"You've never been here, have you?" Jillian replied.

"You know I don't like the outdoors," Allie reminded. "Every time you were coming down here, it sounded hot and dirty and outdoors."

Jillian nodded in agreement at her friend's description. "It was, but it was also a grand adventure. If we want to find anything interesting tonight, we need to get away from the crowd if we can. There are too many people around Craig Mound. I thought we could walk up the path that parallels the field and check out the area around Brown Mound, the temple mound. It's only partly excavated, and maybe it's quieter."

Sure enough, with every step they took approaching Brown Mound, the crowd thinned. Finally, Jillian looked down the grassy field and pointed at the many bobbing lights. "Look, Allie, from here, they look like human lightning bugs."

"They do. The grounds are bigger than I expected."

"There are many mounds in the area, and some of them aren't even in the park. Craig Mound and Brown Mound are the biggest, but Craig Mound is more famous. I thought we'd hang out away from the crowd."

"Good idea," Allie said. They heard an owl hoot in the distance. "That sounds like Halloween. I know there are owls around Magnolia Hill, but I hardly ever hear them."

"I'm glad you came," Jillian said. "Let's go off to the side of Brown Mound, in the back. When Spiro was a thriving Mississippian community, the wealthy lived in a row of houses there. If nothing else, it's an easy place to walk around out of view because of all the trees."

As Jillian and Allie stepped off the asphalt and into the grass, Jillian was glad she wore her sturdy boots. Now that they were at the edge of the trees, the moonlight created crazy shadows while leaves on the ground hid branches and holes. She glanced over at

Allie, who was carefully watching where she stepped. The owl hooted again, and the breeze loosened some of the drying leaves from the branches and sifted them down. When a drifting leaf hit Allie's head, she jumped and looked up with wide eyes.

Jillian didn't want to admit the scene was spookier than she had anticipated. She didn't intend to go far into the woods. Instead, she wanted to get out of sight and watch what was happening from a distance. Unlike Allie, Jillian wasn't afraid of being attacked by a spirit, but she wasn't sure who else could be near them in the dark. She was sure the blue lights were a hoax, a Halloween trick designed to draw attention to the mounds. If she could, she'd like to debunk the myth. Of course, if the ghosts were real, she didn't want to miss seeing them either.

She turned to where she knew Allie was standing and could see her friend's features move in and out of the light. She steadied her voice. "Assuming the mounds aren't haunted, I wonder why someone is trying to draw attention to them. I'm sure most people watching the national morning shows never heard of Spiro before today."

Allie peered farther into the forest and visibly shivered. "I don't know what I think. A hoax could be a stupid trick, an effort to draw attention to the mounds, or a marketing strategy to bring more diners into a new, fandangled pizza place in Spiro."

"Fandangled pizza? That's not an Italian name," Jillian said. "I know what you mean, though. Maybe it's only a creative way to draw attention to something here in town. It's working. I bet the local restaurants are thanking the ghost for their best night all year."

"You know it," agreed Allie. "Hey, can we go back?

I don't like walking in the dark, especially when the open grassy field is so nice and bright from the moon. And I don't even own hiking boots." Jillian flashed her phone light down to Allie's feet and saw dusty high-top sneakers.

"Yeah, let's head back." Jillian sighed. "I guess we aren't going to see anything." The owl hooted again. Suddenly, she stumbled over something. She almost fell, and her hand hit the ground. Except it wasn't ground. In spite of herself, she whimpered.

"Allie, I've fallen over something, and I don't think it was a log," she whispered, realizing that walking in the woods had been an incredibly bad idea.

Allie flashed her phone down on the ground, and both women screamed when they saw an arm sticking out from the leaves.

Chapter Ten

As she was screaming, Jillian heard the sound of crunching leaves and snapping twigs coming from deeper in the woods. She sucked in a huge breath of air and forced her hand to lift her phone and shine it into the darkness. In the shadows, she saw someone running away, and she grabbed Allie's arm and pointed. Her light caught flashing reflections of fluorescent blue. They certainly weren't flames from a spirit. Could they be paint on a jacket?

Jillian wanted to pursue the figure, but she couldn't make her legs move. After her initial shock, she also couldn't speak. She stood, splitting her gaze between the now quiet woods and the arm exposed in the pile of leaves. Allie's legs and voice worked just fine, however, and she ran out into the grass clearing and repeatedly screamed "Help!" at the top of her voice.

As bobbing lights approached, Jillian knew someone would call the police. Morbid curiosity made her use her hoodie sleeve to gently move away more of the leaves. She gasped as Fred Winkler's face emerged, his Einstein hair wildly strewn around his too-still face. She thought she saw blood under his head and wondered if something or someone struck him. She backed away from his body as nausea overwhelmed her. She hurried back to the clearing on the other side of Brown Mound, bent over close to the ground, and lost her dinner. She used her boot to cover it with twigs and dirt.

When she glanced back, gawkers were already gathering around Fred's body, and Jillian yelled out for no one to touch anything. The crowd looked over at her. A few people appeared aggravated that she would be giving orders, some began to cry, while others stepped away sickened by the sight. Most stared down, frozen by a horror they had never seen before.

Jillian heard the soft sound of a siren growing louder and louder. She quietly walked out to the path by the trees and sat down cross-legged on the asphalt. Allie, tears streaming down her cheeks, sat down beside her. "It's Fred," Jillian whispered.

"How awful." Allie choked on her words, and Jillian took her hand.

"I know," she said, suddenly exhausted. The loud sirens stopped, and two police officers were almost to Craig Mound, so she stood back up and walked over to them. One officer was tall and thin, while his partner was short and round. She explained the day's events to them, including how she and Allie found the body.

The short officer sounded suspicious. "So you're telling us that you just happened to come to the exact spot in this whole area," he swept his pudgy arm around the massive site, "where you found the body of someone you happen to know?"

The tall officer gave Jillian an apologetic smile. "Well, it was quite a coincidence."

Jillian sighed. "I know. But remember, I told you my father's an archeologist, and I've been on digs at this site through the years. That's why I came down here. My dad told me that Fred Winkler wanted to talk to him, and I thought it might have something to do with the blue lights."

Both men's shoulders sank at her final words. "Yes, the blue lights," the taller officer grumbled. "I guess they're good for tourism, but they've kept us busy since the original story broke a few days ago."

If poor Fred hadn't been lying in the leaves, Jillian would have asked more questions about the supposed haunting. However, given the circumstances, she thought she should keep the conversation moving in a direction that gave the officers confidence she wasn't a killer.

"I'm sure it's been difficult. My father never got a chance to talk to Fred about his concerns. Once he and my mom arrived in Spiro this morning, he called him. Fred said he wanted to talk to him in the afternoon, away from the mounds. For the rest of the day, Dad called and called, but it went to voicemail. He even checked with the guards at the site to see if they knew anything. I guess we know what happened now."

The pudgy officer spoke again. "Remind me how you know the body is Fred." His tone sounded like he hadn't believed anything Jillian said.

Jillian's face flushed. "I moved a few leaves. I wrapped my hand in my hoodie, so I wouldn't leave fingerprints." The round officer nodded, and both of his chins bobbed up and down. "Anyway, I uncovered his face, and I saw it was Fred."

"You're sure?"

"I've known him since I was a little kid. I always thought he resembled Einstein, with his hair flying all over the place. Yes, I'm sure it's Fred Winkler."

While Jillian was talking, the tall officer walked

over to the body and kept everyone away. Jillian heard more sirens approaching and figured all the bystanders would be moved shortly.

"Do you need anything else from me?" she asked.

"I don't know," the round officer said. "Probably, but it can wait until tomorrow." His tone had become more gentle, and his expression lost some of its suspicion. He looked at her with pity, and Jillian was amazed at how kindness transformed his features. Maybe he believed her.

"You can prove everywhere you've been until you came into the park, right?" he asked.

"Yes, Officer. The motel receptionist talked to me when I checked in. So did the waitress at the diner."

"Why don't you both head back to the motel? We'll need time to process the scene. We may need to talk to you again. Will you be around?"

"That sounds a lot like a movie line, 'Don't leave town,' " Jillian said.

"It does, but I didn't mean it that way," the officer said with a small smile. "But I might need to get some clarification from you tomorrow."

"No problem," Jillian said. "You've got my cell phone number and where I'm staying. Please let me know if I can do anything to help."

"Right now, why don't you girls go back? Are you okay to drive?"

Jillian nodded. She and Allie started walking back to the car, along with the crowd of people who no longer wanted a ghost hunt. Everyone was mostly silent. A few people were still crying. The owl hooted again.

Almost to herself, Jillian said, "I sure hate to wake up Dad with this news."

Chapter Eleven

Jillian didn't want to tell her father about Fred's death over the phone. This was the sort of news that needed to be given in person. As she crossed the bridge again, she turned back to the site. The fun spookiness was gone, and in its place, true fear showed on the faces of people following them out.

The red and blue flashing police lights made Jillian a little dizzy as she and Allie walked through the parking lot to the truck on the street. Once they were both buckled in, Jillian waited for a break in the traffic to pull out. Everyone in the county appeared to be driving down the road in front of the site.

As cars were streaming past, Jillian looked over at the round bales of hay in the field beside the park. The nearly full moon shined down so brightly she could see the red, white, and blue mesh wrapping around what resembled giant-sized jelly rolls.

She didn't use round bales with Agatha because her mare trashed the hay, tearing off large sections without eating it. The waste made it an expensive option.

Jillian jumped when Allie's voice brought her away from her thoughts of the barn. "Jilly, do you think we saw Fred's killer running away in the woods?"

"I don't know," Jillian admitted. "I hope not, but I don't know who else it would be. Why would someone else be in the woods near his body?"

"I don't know. That's scary." Allie drew her knees up on the seat.

"It is. Did you see the glowing blue splotches on his clothes?"

"They reminded me of my shirts when I've made a mess."

"I'm not calling you messy, but I agree." Allie hit her gently on the arm, and Jillian continued. "His shirt was splattered with fluorescent paint. I bet he's the person behind the recent ghost sightings."

Allie glanced over at her, a combination of relief and disappointment on her face. "Then the ghost isn't real?"

"I'm afraid not, friend. Poor Fred. I bet he was suspicious about the bobbing lights and went into the woods to investigate. Apparently, the hoaxer didn't want to get caught." The flashing police lights were making Jillian more dizzy, and her nausea returned. Finding a body probably didn't help either.

"I can see a Halloween prank," Allie said slowly. "But how was that worth killing somebody? And if Fred was recently killed, where was he all day?"

Jillian shook her head. "I don't know. I would think the worst punishment for pretending to be a ghost would be a slap on the hand and maybe a fine for entering the park after hours."

"Like we did?" Allie asked.

"That was different. We were investigating," Jillian said, taking a justified tone. Finally, the traffic began to thin. "Come on. I'm ready to get out of here."

As she started to pull away, Jillian's phone rang, and she saw Will's picture on her caller ID. She used her truck's automated system and pressed the green button on the screen. "Hey. Why are you calling so late?"

Will's normally strong voice sounded frightened. "People always want to make sure reporters have heard the latest gossip. I got an email from a friend who told me that a body was found at the Spiro mounds."

"I know. We found it," Jillian said quietly.

"You found it?" Will sounded incredulous. "How did you do that? Who was it? Are you okay? Where was it?" As he started to ask something else, Will's staccato questions made Jillian even more dizzy.

"Slow down, please," Jillian asked. "I'll tell you everything, but I'm a little overwhelmed. It was my father's friend, Fred Winkler. He's the one my mom and dad came down here to see, but he never came to the meeting with my dad this afternoon. I haven't told my folks about his death yet. They're going to be devastated." Jillian was happy for the string of cars in front of her. The road to the site wasn't brightly lit, but the traffic made it easy to see the way.

"I'm so sorry," Will said. "Are you okay? How did you find him?"

"I guess I'm okay, sort of. Allie's with me. We were trying to figure out the blue light hoax. Honestly, I'm lying. I'm not fine. It was awful. I literally tripped over his body."

"I'm so sorry. You can't possibly be okay. Could you see how he died? Did someone kill him?"

"Based on the amount of blood I saw under his head, I think somebody hit him."

Will gave a low whistle. "So you think he was murdered? Where are you now?"

"Headed back to the motel. The police want to talk to me again tomorrow, so we'll be here a couple of days."

"Do you want me to come down there?" Will asked.

"You don't have to do that. I'll be fine. I'm with my folks and Allie."

"You know I don't mind. You're not still mad, are you?"

Jillian's heart ached. "Of course not. I'm not mad at you, Will. Let me know if you hear anything else. Love you," she whispered.

"Love you more. I'll call you in the morning."

"Love you, too," Allie sang out, and everyone was relieved to laugh.

After Will hung up, Allie smiled over at Jillian. "See? Even though the evening has been horrible, I told you that you guys needed to make up. He was worried about you."

"I know," Jillian said, and for the second time that day, she pulled into the parking lot of the motel. They got out of the truck, and Jillian's apprehension left her legs and heart heavy as she approached her parents' room. Finally, she took a deep breath and knocked on the door.

Chapter Twelve

Shortly after she quietly rapped on her parents' door, she called out to them softly. "Mom, Dad, it's me." She heard them moving around inside.

"Jillian?" her father finally called out.

"Please open the door," she said.

"Hang on a second. I'll be right there." As Jillian stood outside, tears streamed down her cheeks.

Finally, her dad opened the door. "Jillian, Allie, what's wrong? Come inside." As she entered, she smelled the same stale cigarette smoke that permeated her room. Her mom sat on the edge of the king-sized bed. She'd pulled an ancient, cigarette-burned blanket around the shoulders of her pajamas.

Jillian sat down beside her, and Allie sat on the end of the bed. Jillian tried to speak, but she couldn't get her voice above a whisper.

"Oh, Dad, Mom, I don't know how to say it. Fred's dead."

Her father sank into the chair beside the table. "What? No, you must be wrong. I talked to him this morning."

Allie shook her head sadly while Jillian reached forward to put a hand on his arm. "I'm not wrong. We found his body in the trees beside Brown Mound."

Tears filled her father's eyes. "I can't believe it.

What were you doing beside Brown Mound when the lights were seen at Craig?"

Jillian's voice shook as she tried to speak. She couldn't make eye contact with her dad, so she focused on some blue pen stains on the surface of the ancient Formica table. "Well, you know, Allie and I were going to try to figure out how someone created the blue orbs. Craig Mound was swarming with ghost hunters. I thought if we moved away from the crowd, we might be able to see something in the distance that wasn't as obvious when people were closer."

"Smart," he said.

"I guess." Jillian sighed. "But I wish now I hadn't done it. I tripped over him." The shock of the event left her speechless for a moment as her mother and father stared at her. "I guess someone hit him on the back of the head and then covered him with leaves. I feel so bad. I didn't see him until I was on top of him. I didn't mean to step on him." She began to cry.

"I know you didn't." Her mom put her arm on her shoulders, and the tears streamed down Jillian's face harder. "I feel awful about Fred, but I also feel terrible that you went through that. Are you okay?"

"I guess. I've talked to the police and told them everything. I also think we might have seen the person responsible for the glowing orbs."

"Where?"

"Running away from Fred's body. Poor Fred. After all that he's contributed to archeological research, especially at Spiro. I can't believe someone would kill him over a stupid prank."

Jillian's dad didn't look like he heard anything she said. He simply stared down at his hands. Her mom got up, stood behind his chair, and put her arms around him and across his chest before he started talking.

"I wonder if that's what he wanted to talk to me about. It doesn't make sense. He sounded distressed. This isn't the first time people have been caught pulling ghost pranks down here, especially around Halloween. I don't know why he would have been so upset about it. And if you're right, and his killer was running away, you might have barely missed the murder."

Her father shuddered, and her mother's arms tightened around him before she spoke. "I'm so glad you girls are safe. I never thought anything could happen to you looking for imaginary ghosts. You could have been killed, too." Jillian never considered that. Fred's death rattled her so much that she hadn't thought about danger for her or Allie. Her nausea of earlier returned.

From the end of the bed, Allie squeaked, "Broomsticks."

"I still don't understand it. Fred figures out the hoax, lures the guy into the woods after dark, and the hoaxer kills him?" Jillian's dad asked again. "The timeline doesn't make sense. Where was he all afternoon?"

"Maybe Fred was looking for more evidence before he made an accusation. You know, Will talks to me about murder cases he covers. I'm always horrified at why people kill each other," Jillian said. "When you watch the news or those crime shows, most of the time, it's something stupid."

"I want to talk to the police officers and the guards on duty tonight," her father insisted.

"I don't think they'll let us into the park. There were cops everywhere, and they made us all leave. I think with your credentials, you might be able to get into the

Visitor's Center tomorrow morning, but probably not earlier."

Her father sighed. "Right. I'll wait, but I want to know what happened."

"The police thought they might want to talk to Allie and me some more tomorrow. I don't think we're suspects, but it was pretty chaotic tonight."

Jillian's dad walked absent-mindedly over to the tray on the dresser and unwrapped the cellophane off a flexible plastic water glass. Then, he went to the ancient bathroom sink with corroded fixtures, filled the glass with water, and walked back into the bedroom. He took a sip, made a face, and set the glass back down. He looked over at Jillian.

"Even though I'm shocked, I'm glad you told me about Fred's death tonight. You two should go on back to your room."

You've got to be exhausted," Jillian's mother continued.

"We can stay here with you guys if you want us to," Allie offered.

"No, we'll be fine. We'll see you in the morning. Try to get some sleep."

As Jillian and Allie walked through the parking lot back to their room, Jillian was relieved to breathe clean air for a few minutes. She sniffed the sleeve of her hoodie, and she caught more of the stale smell. People must have been smoking in the motel rooms recently.

She locked the thumb bolt and fastened the chain on the door to their room. She was so tired she just kicked off her shoes, pulled back the bedspread, and lay down on her own ancient blanket. The minute she closed her eyes, she saw Fred's face, wispy hair, and the stain under his head. Why would anyone have done that to such a nice man? She couldn't imagine, and her nausea returned. She didn't know how she would get any rest.

After a long silence, Allie whispered, "Are you still awake?"

"Yes, I don't think I'm going to be able to get any sleep."

"Do you think Fred was murdered right before we got there?"

"I don't know. It looks that way."

"I'm scared. You don't think the guy in the woods saw us, do you?"

"No, I'm sure he didn't. After all, we wore ball caps and hoodies, and he was running away. I didn't see him turn around."

"Besides, he wouldn't know us, right?" Allie continued.

"Right. We're not in any danger. Do you want me to turn on the television for some background noise?"

"That's a good idea," Allie agreed.

Jillian searched for the ancient television remote. She had heard they were the dirtiest parts of hotel rooms. Yuck. Her hand sanitizer was in her makeup bag in the bathroom, so she held the remote as gingerly as possible and carried it into the other room. After a good spritz, she flipped past the shopping channel, a classic movie channel, and the game show channel. She was about to turn the set back off when a news video caught her attention. To her horror, she saw a distant shot of her and Allie talking to the police.

A repeat of the ten o'clock news was discussing a murder at Spiro mounds. Although the reporter didn't know the names of the women who found the body, he promised to update viewers as the station got more information.

"So much for being anonymous," Jillian said, and Allie pulled the sheets over her head.

Chapter Thirteen

Shortly after she finally fell asleep, Jillian woke to "The Good, The Bad, and the Ugly" whistling on her cell phone. She groped around for it in the dark and was surprised when she saw Will's picture on the caller ID.

"Will! What's wrong?"

"I don't want to panic you, but I saw your picture on the news last night," he whispered in a low voice.

Jillian disentangled herself from the ancient blanket on her bed. "I know. Allie and I saw it, too, on a replay of the Fort Smith late news."

"I didn't want you to deal with it by yourself, so I drove down here. I'm outside in the motel parking lot, but I don't know your room number."

Jillian stumbled out of bed and pulled the long white pole that controlled the position of the olive-green curtains and their white plastic liner.

Morning light streamed into the room, and Allie groaned, pulling her second pillow over her head.

Jillian saw Will's multi-colored Mustang in the parking lot. He was in the middle of refurbishing it, and the paint job would be the last step of his process. He shaded his eyes with a hand as he searched for her in the window, and she waved at him. "Wow. I didn't expect you to do that. Give me a second, and I'll come down."

"Okay, take your time."

Jillian hung up the phone and washed her hands and face using a tiny bar of bland-smelling soap wrapped in plastic. Then, she put on clean jeans and a sweatshirt hawking financial software that she picked up for free at a conference. She pulled on clean white socks and her hiking boots, not knowing what the day would bring. She pulled her hair back in a ponytail, slicked on some lip gloss, and headed for the motel door.

"Allie, get some more sleep. Will's driven down, so I'm going to go outside and talk to him. We might run to the diner to get some coffee."

"Mmm hmm," Allie agreed and buried herself deeper under the covers.

As Jillian jogged down the concrete stairs, she texted her father, hoping his phone was on vibrate. She was sure he had slept little after learning of Fred's death, and she hoped he didn't know that she and Allie were on the news.

Will stood outside his car by the time she got down the stairs. He opened his arms, and she stepped into them. She knew he couldn't do anything to keep her safe, but his presence gave her confidence, and this morning, that was enough. He gave her a quick kiss on the forehead and pulled her face back to look at her. His eyes were red, likely from lack of sleep and a night of driving.

"Are you okay?" he asked.

She shrugged, noticing the scent of his cologne on her shirt. "I guess. As good as I can be."

"I'm sure," Will agreed.

"I can't believe we found Fred's body. I've loved him my whole life. Why would someone want to kill him?"

"I don't know. I suspect it has something to do with

the reported blue lights," Will said. "But honestly, that doesn't seem like enough reason to kill someone."

"My dad thought the same thing last night. Would you like me to drive us to get some coffee? I didn't get much sleep, but I got more than you did." She put an arm around his waist.

"That would be nice. After we talked and I saw your picture on the news, I couldn't go to sleep. I finally gave up and drove down here."

"I bet the last part of the drive was pretty lonely."

"It was, but that made it easier. At least I didn't have the traffic jams you and your dad had to deal with. I've been in the parking lot since about 4:00. I got a couple of hours of sleep before I called you, but I knew you'd want to get an early start to the day."

"I do, and I know Dad does, too. I'll send him another text to tell him that we're at breakfast. He can contact us after he wakes up. I'm sure last night was impossible for him to sleep."

Chapter Fourteen

Jillian and Will were both so tired that they didn't talk much as they ate homemade biscuits and white gravy with sausage served on ceramic plates with enormous mugs of coffee. Jillian thought the tasty gravy was likely what she had eaten the night before with her dinner. Good white homemade gravy was hard to make, but this diner had the process refined to an art form. They were nearly finished when Will reached across the table and took her hand.

"Jillian, I know today is going to be about the death of Fred, but I want to talk to you about Amber for a minute before things get crazy."

For a second, Jillian panicked, but then Will gave her hand a squeeze. She started breathing again. "Will, I trust you. Really, I do. You don't have to tell me anything."

"No, we haven't been fair to you. Or at least I haven't been. Amber reached out to me a few weeks ago, and she was terrified." Jillian raised her eyebrows.

"What was wrong?" she asked before taking a long drink of her coffee.

"Do you remember how Josh's dad threatened me if I ever told anyone about his son's problems?"

Jillian murmured a neutral response. She didn't like Josh, but she didn't want to sound critical. Will told her the story of Josh's problems over the summer, and Jillian believed that Will's friend would never take responsibility for himself until he learned his actions had consequences.

"Well, I guess somehow his dad found out that Amber and I talked, and now he's bullying her, saying he'll get her fired from her job if she says anything critical about Josh."

"That's crazy," Jillian exclaimed. "He can't call her place of work and tell them to fire her. Why is he still obsessing about what happened that far in the past?"

"He's old school, and he's arrogant," Will said. "He also doesn't understand that addiction happens in all families." He gave a disgusted snort. "Because he's a bank president, he holds himself and his family, including Josh, in high esteem, and he expects the rest of us to be impressed, too."

"I guess so," Jillian said. "That's why I don't bank there. How does she expect you to fix it?" She emptied her coffee cup and nodded at the waitress, who appeared with a fresh, fragrant pot. Today, there wasn't enough coffee in the world.

"Amber doesn't know what to do. She wants him to leave her alone, and she hoped that I might know something that would help."

"You mean like information about him?"

"No, of course, she didn't want me to blackmail him. I think she thought because of my friendship with Josh, I might have a relationship with the family. You know I don't."

He added some cream to his coffee and stirred. "She was distraught, so she reached out to me as an old friend, not romantically. That's all it was. I'm sorry. Neither of us wanted to upset you, but she asked me not to talk about it."

Will's leg was jiggling up and down so hard he was moving the table. Jillian knew the encounter and her reaction to it stressed him.

"I understand. I just wish you trusted me enough to know I wouldn't talk about something like that." She didn't want to sound angry, but she was sad that he didn't understand her better.

"Oh, I trust you. I promise I do. She asked me not to talk about it."

When Jillian started to respond, he cut her off. "I know. I'm not good at talking about things, but you've got to admit, I'm getting better," he said hopefully.

"You are, and I need to be more trusting." When his eyes clouded, she continued, "It's not that I don't trust you. I do. I think I worry way too much. I need to let things go sometimes."

"Probably, but that isn't who you are. Anyhow, that's all it is. I wish we could get him to leave her alone, but for now, she's ignoring him." He wiped up the last of the gravy with his biscuit.

"Maybe she should talk to her boss," Jillian offered.

"I suggested that, but she thinks it will make things worse."

Before she could say anything else, Jillian's phone rang, and she saw her dad's picture appear on her caller ID. "Oh, Dad's awake. Let me get this."

Chapter Fifteen

After Jillian got off the phone, Will paid for breakfast, and they went back to the motel. Her dad was waiting for them outside.

"Hi, you two. Will, thanks for making the trip down here." He reached out to shake Will's hand, but Will drew him into a hug.

"After I talked to Jillian, I couldn't get back to sleep."

"I guess my age is showing," her father admitted. "I laid awake for a while, but then I passed out. I was exhausted. I'd like to go to the site this morning and see if we can find anything out."

"Does Mom know you left?" Jillian asked.

"I told her, but she was mostly asleep. I left a note on the table in the room. I think she was awake longer than me, and she's on the verge of a migraine. If she can get some rest, she might ward it off, so I don't want her to get up yet."

"Poor Mom. I hope she feels better soon. Allie's also not a morning girl, so I told her I was leaving, but I also left a text message. When she really wakes up, she'll know where I am. I don't think she's anxious to go back to Spiro this morning. Last night was scary."

"Sweetie, I wouldn't have suggested you come down here if I thought there was any real danger. Fred sounded upset, but I thought he was irritated about the hoax." Her father's voice broke, he took a deep breath, and he wiped an eye with the back of his hand. "That's why I'm anxious to go talk to people at the site this morning."

"Please don't feel guilty. You couldn't have expected any of this. Why don't you let me drive," Jillian suggested.

When she pulled her truck into the parking lot of the Spiro Visitor's Center, she saw several news vans, two police cars, and a few other vehicles. Once inside, the memories flooded over Jillian as she looked around at displays that had been there for years. The Center employees had also created room for several new cabinets holding the traveling exhibit. Her father walked toward a plump woman with silver hair and a face remarkably absent of wrinkles. Her blue eyes were red and puffy, and when she saw Jillian's dad, she rushed over to him, away from the two officers near her.

"Oh, Robert, he's dead," she sobbed.

He gave her a comforting hug. "Marlene, meet my daughter Jillian and her friend Will. Jilly, Marlene Jenner worked with Fred, Don, me, and several other scientists to organize the traveling exhibition."

"Nice to meet you," said Jillian, offering the woman a hug. Marlene clung to Jillian tightly before she let go.

"You don't remember me, but I knew you when you were a young girl. You used to come down here in the summer." The memory caused Marlene to offer a small smile.

"I did," Jillian agreed. "This was one of my favorite places when I was growing up."

"You wouldn't have any reason to remember me. I

was just another adult digging here. I wasn't fun like Fred or your dad," she said sadly.

"This was your job," Jillian reminded her. "I'm sorry for your loss." Marlene's eyes filled with tears again.

"I was telling the officers I can't imagine why anyone would have killed Fred," she explained. The two policemen had stepped back to allow everyone to talk, but they rejoined the group when they were mentioned.

Neither of them were the men Jillian and Allie spoke with the night before. Maybe nearby towns were also assisting, as Jillian couldn't imagine Spiro having a large force.

"We were talking to Dr. Jenner about Dr. Walker's role and any recent unusual activity at the center or the site," one of the officers said.

Marlene twisted and untwisted a tissue in her hand. "I told them that Fred was more absent-minded than usual the last few days, and he was snappy with the volunteers. You know that wasn't like him, Robert. I blamed it on the exhibit. We've all been worried about the safety of the artifacts even though we have extra security." She nodded briefly at the guards at the front door and the side door that led to the path going into the site. Then, she faced Jillian's dad again.

"When you called me yesterday looking for Fred," her voice broke, and she stopped for a moment. "I started thinking more. We knew about the blue light hoax before it made the news. Fred may have been more upset about the notoriety than I thought. He was fun, but he took the science seriously. He didn't want the mounds to turn into a Halloween attraction."

Jillian remained silent, unwilling to tell the sincere

woman that she was one of the ghost hunters. Of course, she probably already knew if she had watched the evening news and seen the video. Instead, she nodded in agreement. "I'm sure you didn't want people making a joke out of everything you'd worked so hard to bring together."

Will spoke up. "Do you have any idea who might have been creating the blue lights?"

Marlene snorted. "You ought to ask Todd Block. He has a podcast where he talks about all the ghosts he claims he found around here. He calls it Okie Spirits, and he's been obsessed with Spiro recently, interviewing people who have seen the lights. He even claims he can communicate with ghosts from this area." The police officers tried to hide their smiles, but Jillian's dad made no such effort and laughed out loud.

"Is Todd still on that kick? He's been obsessed with the supernatural since high school. He'd try to come out to the site even then with spirit boxes and other ghost-detecting equipment. I figured he'd given up on all that."

Chapter Sixteen

As Jillian's father offered his opinion of Todd, the podcaster, she watched Will typing on his phone. She knew he was writing down the name of the influencer and his show. Maybe they could talk to him later in the day. If Todd was obsessed with the local ghost stories, maybe he would have some ideas about the blue lights. And if he was creating the hoax, maybe Fred found him in the woods, and Todd panicked and hit him over the head.

Jillian briefly considered sharing her ideas with the two police officers, but she decided against it. She knew she was just guessing, and law enforcement didn't appreciate that.

Instead, she asked her dad, "How well do you know Todd Block?"

"Not very," her father admitted. "He was a bright enough kid, but he's sounded like a carnival barker for years. I guess I shouldn't be surprised that he has convinced people he's an influencer." He paused and glanced over the top of his glasses, first at Jillian, then at Will. "How do you make money as an influencer?"

Jillian considered trying to explain monetization to her father. He was smart enough to understand it. Heck, he was probably the smartest person she knew, but he wouldn't understand how people created value that way.

Instead, she smiled and said, "I'm not sure. I think he gets money because he's a content creator."

"A content creator?" Jillian's dad shook his head. "I've written five books. That's content. Seems like a 'money for nothing' scheme if you ask me. I don't see a lot of value in pretending you can talk to ghosts."

Jillian gave him a quick hug. "I know."

"I only want to know who killed Fred."

Marlene let out a choked yelp. "Me, too," she agreed. The woman looked so distressed that Jillian wanted to give her a chance to talk to her dad alone. After all, Fred and the two of them had been colleagues and friends for years.

"Dad, while you guys talk, do you mind if Will and I go outside and look around?"

"Don't disturb the crime scene," the police officer warned.

"We won't," she promised. They murmured goodbyes as they went out the door that led to the mounds.

Once they were outside, Jillian started walking rapidly toward the bridge. Will had been looking around, and he jogged a couple of steps to catch up. He took Jillian's hand. "What are you doing?"

"I think the person I saw running away killed Fred. I want to go back and see if he dropped anything or left something to prove he was there."

"Don't you think the police have already searched the area?" Will questioned. "They won't want us nosing around the crime scene."

"We won't disturb anything." She ignored Will's questioning glance. "I know you wouldn't, but I won't either," she corrected. "I want to figure out what happened to Fred."

"I think the local authorities are better equipped to deal with this, and I'm sure before the day is over, the Oklahoma State Bureau of Investigations will also be here. They often become involved in serious cases that happen in smaller towns."

"That's probably a good protocol," Jillian said, but she didn't break her stride. "If we find anything, we won't touch it."

With Craig Mound in the distance, Jillian and Will carefully walked to Brown Mound until they reached the police tape perimeter. Even at a quick glance, the location of Fred's body was obvious. The ground had been cleared of leaves, and a brown stain soaked the earth. Jillian couldn't stand it, so she moved toward where she thought she saw the figure running. She was glad the police had only taped off the location of the body, but she suspected the whole area was really the crime scene.

She searched along the ground and even up on the tree trunks and low-hanging branches. Everything looked the same. After she had scoured the area, she sighed in frustration. "With all the debris and leaves, maybe I'm wasting my time. I don't even know what I'm looking for." She glanced at Will. "I thought maybe I could find a piece of fabric or something."

Will looked up from the forest floor. "You mean like in a murder mystery?" he said. "Real clues aren't that obvious, and anything like that would already have been found by the police. They're good at their job."

"I know. But could we look a little longer, just in case?" she pleaded to Will until she saw a small smile.

"Okay," Will agreed. "You keep going the same

direction, and I'll go back the other way in case our runner dropped something before they either killed or found Fred. You know, they might not be the murderer. Finding a body might have scared someone enough to make them run away.

Jillian walked slowly, looking for a scrap of something. Now that she was off the path, the leaves covered everything. She started kicking them with her toe like she did when she was small. She smiled as the leaves flew off the end of her hiking boot, and occasionally, a small twig would launch. Then, her foot made contact with something harder, and at first, she thought she kicked a rock. She walked up to the item for a closer look and gasped. A beautifully decorated, ancient bowl lay at her feet, and one side was covered in a brown substance that Jillian thought was dried blood.

Chapter Seventeen

Jillian stood, frozen for a second, looking at the ancient weapon. "Will," she called. "Come here. Look what I found."

She heard him approaching but couldn't tear her gaze from the item lying on the leaves. She heard him give a low whistle. "What is that?" he asked.

"It looks like a Mississippian-period bowl. And I think it has blood on one side."

"How did you find it?"

"I kicked it. I don't want to touch it. Let's go back and get the police."

"No, you stay here. I'll go back. I don't want us to lose it, and everything out here looks alike."

"Good idea," Jillian agreed. As Will's steps grew fainter, a gust of wind released dead leaves that drifted to the ground, partially covering the bowl. She was glad Will suggested someone stay at the location, although she wished she had been the one to go back. The ghost hunters were long gone, and no one was in the park. Jillian realized it was probably closed to the public until the police finished. Even though she could see the clearing, the woods were spooky.

"Now, Jillian, don't let your imagination run away with you," she scolded herself. She knew that Fred's murderer was long gone and wasn't likely to return

during daylight with so many police officers in the Visitor's Center. Of course, that assumed the murderer wasn't someone who worked at the site and was sitting in the building Will was approaching. She couldn't imagine one of the archeologists using a priceless relic as a weapon. Did the bowl send a message? Was someone unhappy with the work being done at the site?

Maybe the killer didn't like the traveling exhibit. There were people who wanted the relics reburied into the mounds out of respect, but Jillian's dad told her that he didn't think that would be practical. Spiro fell into a loophole. Because the bodies weren't buried directly with the artifacts, the rules of returning the two together didn't apply. Plus, the site didn't have unlimited resources for elaborate, permanent security. New looting would be inevitable.

Jillian thought about how her time at Spiro had given her an appreciation for the early people who called the area home or visited for trading and religious purposes. She was glad their artifacts were being displayed. She believed showing people the ancient cultures in a respectful way led to a greater appreciation for the intelligence and advanced nature of the First Americans.

Another gust of high wind spread clouds over the sun, and the autumn warmth gave way to a warning of impending winter. In spite of her hoodie, Jillian wrapped her arms around herself and glanced toward the Center nervously. She would be glad when Will returned with the policemen.

Soon, she saw Will, a police officer, and her father walking across the wide lawn. When they reached her, her father took a brush and lightly removed the leaves. "I can't believe you found this," he said with disbelief.

The police officer bent down to pick it up. "Careful," her dad reminded him. "We don't want to damage it." The officer gently put the bowl in an evidence bag and tagged it. Her father looked at it closely.

"How could one of the artifacts get out here?" he asked.

"Could someone have found it?" Will questioned. He took Jillian's hand, and she was grateful for the warmth. "I mean in a recent, unauthorized dig."

"I can't believe that. A few of the mounds aren't excavated, but they are small. Brown Mound is rumored to still have some small artifacts. But if someone found this, it would be a remarkable discovery. Unless it was purely a black market dig conducted in secret, the Oklahoma and Arkansas archeology communities would have heard about it."

As they walked back toward the clearing, Jillian's father pointed over at the tape. "Is that where you found him?" he asked quietly.

Jillian nodded, a lump forming again in her throat.

"I'm sorry you went through that," he said. "I hope he wasn't lying out here long."

The group formed a single-file line as they crossed the narrow bridge. As they continued walking on the gravel path, her dad stared over at the bowl and shook his head.

"I still don't understand why someone would use this to kill Fred. I can't believe it didn't break."

"Maybe Fred and the killer were fighting over it," Will offered. "Could two people have been working together, and one person didn't want to share?"

"It's possible, but I'd be more likely to believe that someone wanted to keep it, and Fred wanted it put into a museum or the display." He reached over, and the officer let him hold the bagged relic. He turned the bowl over and over in his hands. "This is remarkable."

"Could someone have stolen it from the exhibit?" Jillian asked.

"Maybe, but I still don't understand why it would be used as a weapon. Will I have a chance to look at it more closely?" he asked the officer.

"We'll need to determine the brown substance. I don't want to guess, but it looks like dried blood. We can run DNA and see if we get a match to Dr. Winkler or someone else. Once we're done with it, I'm sure you can look at it more closely."

"I'd appreciate that," he said.

"I think we've probably accomplished all we can this morning," Will told Jillian. "You were unbelievably lucky to spot the bowl. Want to go back and get your mom and Allie? I could use another cup of coffee, and I hope they have a room in the motel."

"We have two beds," Jillian's dad said. "I appreciate your coming down here to keep Jilly safe. You're welcome to crash there if you can't find anything else."

"Thanks." They re-entered the Visitor's Center, and Marlene rushed over to look at the bagged artifact.

"I can't believe it," she said. "Why would anyone use something like this as a weapon, let alone to kill Fred?"

"That's what we're going to figure out, ma'am," the officer promised, taking the bag back from Jillian's dad.

As they told Marlene goodbye, promising to return soon, Jillian's father pulled her aside for a moment.

"Please let us know if the police tell you anything about the weapon."

"I will," she said.

Once Jillian, Will, and her father were settled in the truck, her dad leaned the front captain's chair back and closed his eyes.

"Dad, do you want to get some rest? We can drive Mom and Allie to the diner if you're tired."

"No, I'm just closing my eyes for a minute. A little coffee, and I'll be as good as new."

"Okay, but I want you to take care of yourself. You, too, Will. When you don't get much sleep, you're more likely to have an accident."

"Don't forget to take your own advice, but I agree with your dad. I'll feel a lot better after more coffee. Besides, we can't rest. We've got a podcaster to call."

Chapter Eighteen

After a breakfast of biscuits, honey, and ham for Jillian's mom and Allie and gallons of coffee for the others, Jillian and Will dropped everyone else off at the motel. Then, they headed back up the state highway to Sallisaw, where Todd Block, the ghost hunter and podcaster, lived. He had enthusiastically agreed to meet them at a nearby fast-food restaurant even though he claimed he didn't have a lot of time.

Will insisted on driving, and Jillian was secretly relieved. Her poor sleep the night before led to fatigue that was catching up with her. Still, her excitement about talking to Todd gave her energy.

As they stepped into the red and yellow restaurant with a tile floor the color of Oklahoma red dirt, the heavenly smell of French fries revived Jillian. The screaming of the toddlers didn't have the same effect.

She searched the restaurant, and her gaze settled on a young man with dark, spiky hair and square black glasses. His black T-shirt proclaimed, "Love Me, Love My Ghost." She tugged on Will's arm and glanced over at the edgy young man seated at the table, typing away on his laptop covered in stickers of Bigfoot, aliens, and other cryptids. He seemed out of place among patrons in plaid shirts and boot-cut jeans, which were more popular attire. Will nodded at her and approached the table.

"Todd?" The man closed his laptop.

"Will?" he asked.

"Yes, glad to meet you. This is my friend, Jillian. Like I said, I'm a reporter in Magnolia Hill, but that's not why we wanted to talk to you. We heard from Marlene at the Spiro site that you are a local expert on the ghostly sightings in the area." Jillian wasn't sure if Will meant the last statement as a compliment, but Todd smiled broadly.

"And my dad, Robert Bradford, remembers you coming to digs at Spiro when you were younger," she added.

"You're Robert Bradford's daughter? That's cool. Wait a minute. Didn't I also see you on the news last night?"

As Jillian sat on the red, molded plastic chair, her heart sank, but she tried to keep her emotions off her face. "Yes, you did. What a tragedy."

"The reporters said you found the body," Todd continued.

"I did," she admitted. "My friend and I were shocked when we saw ourselves on the news." She wondered if Allie, frightened by the experience, had slept all night with her head under a pillow.

"Why were you outside at night?" Todd sounded curious, not critical, and Jillian found herself liking his enthusiasm. Still, maybe killers could be enthusiastic when they weren't murdering people. She leaned back from the table and looked around before she answered. Sitting beside her was a wailing toddler, barely able to walk. He seemed unhappy with his lack of French fries. She felt the same way, but she needed to try to engage Todd into talking more.

"My friend and I were outside looking for the ghost, like everybody else."

"And did you find it?"

Jillian decided not to mention the figure she saw running through the woods. "No, I didn't. Maybe when we found a dead body and my friend screamed, she scared the ghost away." She tried not to sound sarcastic. Was Jillian imagining it, or did Todd's glance drop from her? She decided to ignore it. She was on so little sleep she didn't trust her own judgment. Plus, she was more interested in what he knew than deciding if he was a suspect.

Todd's enthusiasm quickly returned. "I don't think you could scare a ghost by screaming. Most of them wouldn't feel threatened by you."

"So, we hear you're an expert on the Spiro ghost. Why do you think it's active again?" asked Will. "Actually, before you answer that, can we buy you lunch?"

"Sure. I could go for a burger and fries if you guys are going to eat."

"I never turn down fries," Jillian agreed. "Will, do you need any help?"

"No, I've got it."

Jillian decided to use Will's absence to learn more about Todd. He might talk more freely alone. "You're a podcaster?" she asked.

"I am," he replied. "I have about 250 downloads a week."

Jillian enjoyed listening to podcasts but didn't know the details about hosting them. "That sounds impressive."

"It puts me well into the top twenty-five percent

listenership of all podcasts," he said, glancing at his laptop in a way that suggested he was proud of his accomplishment but didn't want to look arrogant about it.

"Wow. And you podcast about ghosts in Oklahoma?" she asked.

"Spirits, hauntings, haunted history. This is my favorite time of year." Todd pointed to the paper jack-o-lanterns taped to the restaurant windows.

"I bet your listenership goes up."

"It does," he agreed, stopping his discussion as Will returned with the food. Jillian noticed the young boy at the adjoining table had quit crying and was shoveling fries into his mouth as fast as he could. She was envious that he could eat that way without attracting dirty looks.

She carefully put one fry in her mouth, chewed, and swallowed. "Will, Todd has 250 downloads a week on his podcast."

"Wow. It's probably easier to monetize it with all that interest." Will opened a package of catsup for his fries. Jillian thought he must know more about the business of podcasting than she did.

"Man, it's crazy how many people want to help sponsor me. They also buy buttons, hats, and shirts. This is my latest one." He swept both hands down the front of the shirt he was wearing. "The money lets me do more research and find cool locations and events to explore. I like to talk about haunted Oklahoma, but I do regional topics, as well. The spirits at Spiro have always been my favorite."

"About that," Will said as he picked up his burger. "Assuming the ghost is real, why do you think it's active again?"

"Well, the sightings happen from time to time, but they were most intense when the site was being looted back in the 1930s. If I were guessing, the ghost doesn't like the exhibit, or someone is making it angry."

"How would I anger the spirit?" Jillian asked, eating another single fry and pretending for a minute that she believed the ghost might be real.

"The ghost would be mad if it believed its artifacts were being disturbed."

The memory of the bowl covered in blood almost made Jillian choke on her fry even though she was eating it like an adult.

Chapter Nineteen

Jillian hoped that her quick gulp of soda would make Todd believe she only choked on her food, not his words. He was so happy to be telling his story that he didn't seem to notice.

Instead, with a shy grin, he asked, "I don't mind answering your questions, but can I ask you about a couple of things?" He set his burger back into its box.

Jillian wanted to say no, but Will's almost imperceptible nod caused her to change. "Okay," she said.

"I saw you on the news, but the reporters didn't talk about you personally or mention your name. The chyron claimed that you found the body. Is that right?"

Jillian nodded.

Todd's eyes shone with excitement, but he checked himself and quit smiling. "I'm sorry I look enthusiastic. Of course, I'm not glad Dr. Winkler died."

Jillian was curious how Todd knew that Fred was the victim. "Why do you think it was Dr. Winkler?"

Todd answered with a question. "I'm right, aren't I?"

"I'd rather not say," Jillian responded, knowing her answer sounded so lame that she confirmed his belief. "Really, why do you think it was Dr. Winkler?" she asked again.

"A bunch of things. First, I was at the exhibit a couple of days ago, and Dr. Winkler was on the phone arguing with someone. He was hard to hear, but I think he said the artifacts weren't displayed properly. When he saw me looking at him, he turned his back and dropped his voice. Then, there's Marlene."

"Marlene?" Jillian and Will asked together.

Todd gave a smile, appearing to be pleased to have gossip to share. "She's a nice lady and all, but I think she wanted to be extra nice to Dr. Winkler."

"Be careful before you try to spread any gossip," Jillian snapped. "Dr. Winkler and Dr. Jenner are respected professionals." Jillian emphasized the last words, leaving her opinion of Todd's credentials to herself. "He's a friend of mine, and I know he's an ethical man."

"I'm not saying he isn't," Todd agreed. "I'm sorry. I didn't intend to make you angry, but that doesn't mean Marlene wasn't making a play for him. Earlier this week, I was talking to one of the guards, and she told me that Marlene tried to kiss Dr. Winkler, and he pulled away. Apparently, she turned beet red and went into the back room."

"Why would a guard tell you that? How do you know her?"

"I don't know why she told me," Todd admitted. "I figure she's bored. People come to visit, but even with the extensive exhibit, it's pretty quiet."

"That's too bad," Jillian said, realizing Todd was trying to refocus her questions. Why was he creating suspects for Fred's death? Was he trying to throw suspicion away from himself, or was he trying to help? Either way, his information was interesting.

"I know Marlene's worked there forever. I can't imagine that she thought she could make a pass at Dr. Winkler. He has…had…a great marriage." Jillian's eyes filled with unwanted tears as she thought about Suzanne Winkler. His poor widow must be distraught.

"I'm not surprised," Todd said. "Did you ever meet Marlene's husband?"

Jillian shook her head, no, and Todd continued, "What a control freak. He tracked her movements even when she was at work."

"Do you think he had any idea that Marlene was making a move on Dr. Winkler?" Will asked.

"I don't know, but if he did, there'd be trouble. Marlene's husband seemed like the kind of man who would rather solve problems with his fists than a compromise," Todd said, too enthusiastically for Jillian's taste. He must have noticed her expression. He looked away from them and out at the parking lot and Will's car, shrugging his shoulders slightly. "I'm sorry, but I love solving mysteries."

"Well, we can agree on that. I want to know who killed Fred." The minute Jillian spoke, she regretted that she'd admitted he'd been murdered. Wailing coming from the table beside her caught her attention again. The toddler now didn't want to leave the restaurant, and his poor mother was trying to get him to walk upright rather than sliding along the floor as she pulled him by the arm. Finally, she gave up and scooped him into her side. His wailing grew louder and only subsided when the door closed behind them. Poor woman.

Todd seemed to be able to ignore the commotion. He didn't appear surprised to learn that Fred had been murdered and continued breathlessly sharing what he knew. "I've thought something was off for a while. Dr. Winkler's been more stressed out and irritable recently. I assumed it was the exhibit, but now that he's dead, I wonder if it's something else. It could be that the spirits noticed it, too. Or maybe they were making him irritable."

Jillian saw Will roll his eyes and hoped that Todd wouldn't notice it. After a ping, Todd stared at his phone for a minute. Although Jillian usually would have found his behavior rude, she was relieved it captured his attention. She glared at Will and tried to speak kindly.

"So you believe the spirits are upset about the same thing worrying Dr. Winkler?"

Todd pulled himself away from his phone. "Sorry for that. I finally heard back from someone I've been trying to meet, and I'm going to have to leave soon. Answering your question, I strongly suspect that the spirits are angry." Todd sounded so serious that Jillian bit her lip to keep from smiling.

"We appreciate your time. Do you think the same thing worrying the spirits is what got him killed?"

"I don't know. Like I told you, I can think of several people who might have wanted to hurt him. He didn't do anything wrong, though, and I sure hope you catch whoever did it."

"We're leaving that to the police. We wanted to talk to you about the podcast and what you might know."

"Let me know what I can do to help," Todd said.

"We can do that," Will agreed. "Just out of curiosity, what were you doing last night?"

Todd gave a nervous laugh. "You think I killed him? Not me. I was taping an episode of the podcast that's going to be released on Halloween. You know everybody loves a ghost story this time of year."

"So you weren't at the park last night after you taped?"

Jillian thought Todd paled before he answered. "What do you mean?"

"I thought I saw someone with fluorescent paint on a jacket," Jillian said. "I'm not sure the ghost sightings are real."

"And you think I might have staged the hauntings to help my listenership."

"It crossed our minds," Will said steadily.

Todd waited a second too long to answer, and Jillian wondered if he was creating a strong story. "Look," he finally said, "I believe in the ghostly spirits of Spiro. I know some people think it's a hoax, and I can understand why you might wonder if I was responsible for it. But why would I do it?"

"Like you told us, listenership," Jillian answered. "I don't know any other reason. "

"Then, believe me when I told you I wasn't there. Why would I lie to you?" Todd asked. They both shrugged, and after seeing that Jillian wasn't going to ask another question, Todd's enthusiasm returned. "Keep your eyes open at night. I'll bet you have a supernatural experience. The ghosts have something they want you to learn."

Chapter Twenty

Dating a journalist had some advantages, Jillian thought as Will looked up Todd's address in a database. Of course, she probably could have done it online, too, but his system was easier. She and Will sat in his car with the air conditioner limping along and waited for Todd to leave the restaurant. They were going to drive by his house before they headed back to Spiro, and they didn't want him to pull up on them as they were there.

Todd finally left the restaurant, talking on the phone as he walked toward his car. Eventually, he pulled out of the lot and made a left turn. Since Will's paint job was so easy to spot, he stayed several car lengths behind. They knew where they were going, so they stopped half a block away and gave Todd a chance to park and go into his faux-Tudor duplex before they drove by. Jillian was still looking at artificial cross timbers in Will's rear-view mirror when Todd came back outside and tossed something in his big green trash can already at the curb.

"Will, we need to go back around the block," she whispered.

Will slowed down, and confusion showed on his face. "Why are you whispering?"

Jillian smiled and spoke in a normal voice. "I want to tell you a secret, I guess. I need to look in Todd's trash."

"Gross. Why?"

"I just saw him throw something away, and I bet it's related to the Spiro ghost sightings. Why else would he throw an item in the trash that's already at the curb?"

"Because he forgot something?" Will suggested.

"Or he knows we believe he's pulling a hoax, and he's tossing some evidence."

"You sound like you watch too many detective shows, but okay. We'll go back. I thought he seemed a little nervous while he was talking to us."

"I agree," Jillian said. "I think he genuinely liked Fred, but he acted uneasy every time we talked about the ghost."

"You need to be quick. I'm going to pull up on the side street, just around the corner. Do you want to wear a jacket and a hat?"

"It's a little warm for that. I think I'll draw less attention if I just walk normally. If you see anyone watching me, text."

"It would be easier to roll down the window and tell you. I don't think you're stealing something if you take it from the trash, but it might be trespassing. We don't need you getting arrested."

"I'm going to open the lid and glance inside," Jillian insisted.

Will pulled his multi-colored car under a tree. The moving shadows made his paint job less obvious.

Jillian stepped out of the car and waved goodbye. If anyone were looking at her, she was saying goodbye to her boyfriend. She glanced up and down the street as she approached Todd's trash can, which was placed close to the road on the curve so the giant truck could lift and dump it.

As she approached the can, she tried to glance casually at Todd's house. The windowpanes acted like mirrors, so she couldn't see anything, but no one appeared to be watching.

She quickly opened the lid of the can and stepped back as the smell of rancid garbage escaped. Yuck. Her trash didn't smell this bad. Of course, she wasn't a twenty-five-year-old guy who probably ate greasy food. Maybe he also owned a cat. Poor Edgar. He'd resent that assumption.

She took a deep breath of fresh air, stepped back up to the can, and flashed her phone around inside. Something blue shined up at her, and she lowered her arm farther into the can for a closer look. Double yuck. Blue paint glowed when it hit the light from her phone in the dark inside of the can. Some of it was on a paper towel, but more was on a black garment. She motioned for Will to pull up beside her, and as his car approached, she gathered her courage, reached into the nasty can, and grabbed the hoodie with the edge of her T-shirt.

She motioned for Will to roll down his window. "Open your trunk." He popped the lid, and she threw the hoodie in and slammed it shut with a squeak. She jumped into the passenger's seat and glanced back at Todd's house as they pulled away. Had the curtains just moved in Todd's window? Surely, it was her imagination or a reflection. "Drive as fast as you dare." She pulled hand sanitizer out of her purse and sprayed her hands, arms, and the bottom of her shirt. While she continued to spritz, Will cautiously picked up speed on the residential street.

When they were several blocks away, Will slowed again. "What did you find?" he asked.

"A black hoodie with smudges of glowing blue

paint."

Will snorted. "So much for the modern activity of angry, ancient spirits."

"It seems to be a huge coincidence that Todd researches ghosts, reports on glowing blue spirits, and also has glowing blue paint on his jacket," Jillian said. "If he wore a black mask on his face, he'd be almost invisible after dark. The site isn't well-lit," she reminded Will.

"Right," he agreed. "And he does seem to have a genuine interest in the mounds. Maybe he's bringing back the ghosts to stir up interest around the Spiro artifact display."

"Maybe. Certainly, more folks visited the mounds once the sightings were reported. I wonder how many people took the time to visit earlier?"

"I would think the state and national attention would be good for both the park and the display."

"That's right. There was a story on one of the morning shows a couple of days ago."

"Yeah, and the publicity is continuing. Of course, Fred's death is tragic, but people are weird. Sometimes, even bad news attracts a crowd. The AP is still running stories."

"Wow," Jillian said. "Before we give it to the police, I want to show the jacket to Dad. Leave it in your trunk. His trash smelled awful, and you don't need the odor in your car."

"You don't have to tell me that twice. For now, let's head back. Maybe I could grab a quick nap before we all get together for dinner."

"You've got to be exhausted. You know, finding the hoodie in his trash almost proves that Todd is the ghost," Jillian said. "I wonder if he's also the killer."

Chapter Twenty-One

On the drive back to the motel, Jillian's watch buzzed, and she checked the message on her phone. Mister's owner was feeding Agatha, and she sent a message explaining how the mare was reaching over the wall of her stall and eating Mister's hay. The black and white paint knew not to cross her, but he was miserable.

Jillian responded with —*LOL. Poor Mister*— and suggested she give Mister some of Agatha's hay but put it on the other side of his stall. She apologized for Agatha's aggressive behavior but thought moving the food was an easier job than convincing Agatha not to steal it. Mares could be challenging. She shared the exchange with Will, and for a minute, they both got to relax from the stress of faux ghosts and murderers.

Their cheery mood stopped suddenly as they saw flashing lights in the parking lot of the motel. Will whipped into a parking place, and Jillian rushed to her parents' room. The door was standing open. For a second, Jillian feared something had happened to them or Allie.

However, they were all in the room and were fine. They were standing beside the table in a rough circle with two new officers. How many police were down here?

"What's going on?" she asked. "Why are the lights

flashing outside?"

"These officers wanted to ask us, specifically me, a few more questions," her father answered. The stubble of his beard and the weariness in his eyes reminded Jillian again that her dad was growing older.

"The flashing lights scared us to death," Will said.

One of the officers nodded to the other one, who went outside. Soon, the red and blue swirling light in the room ceased.

"Dad, do they want information, or are they questioning you?" Jillian asked.

"It's not questioning," the officer replied stiffly as he rejoined the group. "We don't do official questioning of multiple people in a motel room."

"Still, you came with your lights on," Jillian insisted.

"It's okay," her mom said. "We were able to get the motel receptionist to confirm that we came back here right after dinner last night. I wanted something from the vending machine, and your dad got quarters from the front desk. Then, they talked for quite a while. It gave us an alibi."

"Alibi? You don't need an alibi," Jillian yelped. She faced the two officers. "You two need to leave my parents alone."

Will showed his business card from the *Magnolia Hill Daily*. "Y'all need to quit interrogating these people and get out there and find the real killer."

"We're quite capable of doing our job," the same officer said. "Mr. Bradford," he started.

"Dr. Bradford," Jillian interrupted.

The officer rolled his eyes. "Dr. Bradford," he exaggerated the title, "will you be staying in Spiro for a few more days?"

"I will."

"We won't bother you anymore this evening." He glared at Jillian. "But we may be in touch later," he finished. He walked out of the motel room. The other officer touched his cap briefly and nodded his head as he followed back to their patrol car.

After they left, Jillian and Will told her dad about their conversation with Todd. They walked to Will's car, and he popped his trunk open after three attempts. He shrugged. "It's getting there."

Once the trunk finally opened, Jillian showed her folks the hoodie as she held her nose. "I know we should give this to the police," she said, "but you saw those officers and how quickly they wanted to arrest Dad. I don't trust all of them to do the right thing."

Jillian's mom took a step backward, likely to minimize the smell. "I think they mean well, but they're inexperienced with major crimes."

"Maybe, but what if Todd's the killer, or what if he isn't?" Jillian asked. "He might have only been having some Halloween fun. I'd like to keep the hoodie for a while, and if we get in trouble later, we'll figure something out." She smiled sheepishly at them.

"I always believe in letting the police do their jobs, but I wasn't impressed at how quickly they wanted to wrap this up," Jillian's dad agreed. "But if we're going to keep it, we need to get some rubber gloves and a bag, so we don't contaminate it. Let's get dinner and then find a local dollar store."

"Sounds like a plan," Jillian agreed.

They found a fried chicken chain restaurant and sat at a booth. Even though no one thought they were hungry, they were soon devouring chicken, mashed potatoes, corn, fried okra, and biscuits. For a while, everyone was too busy eating to talk.

"That was good." Will pushed his wooden chair away from the table with a squeak.

"Yeah, I didn't think I could eat, but I guess I was wrong." Allie looked down at the pile of bones on her plate.

"So, Dad, other than the police asking where you were, what else did they want?"

"Nothing. They did promise to let me look at the bowl once they processed it. I'm sure there will be fingerprints since it must have come from the display."

"What a weird choice of weapons. And I think it would have to limit the suspects to people who work down here," Will said.

"Plus, maybe people who owned or managed other collections," Jillian added.

"I don't know," her dad said. "I'm so tired at this point, I can barely think straight. Let's go buy those bags and get some sleep. Will, you got a room, didn't you?"

"I did. Somebody checked out after the murder, so the woman at the front desk gave it to me."

"I'm glad you're here," Jillian said, "but I don't know what we should do next."

Chapter Twenty-Two

Jillian was barely awake when Will's text chirped its arrival the next morning before she got out of bed. — *Come outside as soon as you can.*—

Allie appeared to be asleep, so Jillian quietly threw on some jeans, a clean T-shirt, and flip-flop sandals. She combed her blonde hair, brushed her teeth, and quietly opened the motel door. Allie groaned when the light hit her face, and she rolled over.

"I'll be back soon. Go back to sleep," Jillian whispered to the lump in the bed as she closed the door. She stepped up to the balcony and saw Will standing beside the driver's seat of his car, holding a piece of paper. She started to smile and wave, but then she saw the expression on his face and stopped, calling down to him instead.

"What's wrong?"

Will put a finger to his lips like he was making a hushing sound. He motioned with his other hand for her to come down the stairs, and she took them two at a time, her flip-flops slapping the concrete steps. When she reached his car, he held out the piece of paper.

"I'm sure I should have handled this with gloves, but when I pulled it off my windshield, I had no idea that it would be threatening," he said. "I figured it was an ad for a haunted house or an invitation to attend a local church."

Jillian opened the folded paper. The words were written in big block letters. "Leave or Else!"

Her hand with the paper dropped to her side, and she let go of it. She grabbed it again quickly before the ever-present Oklahoma wind could blow it away.

"I can't believe this. How does someone know you're here, and why are they threatening you?"

Will shook his head from side to side. "I guess someone knows we were looking into Fred's death yesterday, and they want us to stop. He pointed at the brightly colored car. It's not like I blend in."

"We should talk to Dad," Jillian said. "He needs to know he might be in danger, too. Whoever left the note recognized your car and didn't know what the rest of us drove."

She glanced around the parking lot, half expecting to see someone lurking behind the dumpster. "I didn't notice anyone yesterday, did you?"

"You mean other than inviting Todd for burgers?"

"We did that," Jillian admitted. "But we know he was in his house when we drove back."

"True," Will said. "But, in fairness, there aren't many motels around here. He knew we were staying near Spiro. If I wanted to find someone, I'd drive around all the nearby motel parking lots until I found that." He motioned over to his multi-colored car reflecting in the early morning light.

"Whether it was Todd, someone from the Center, or someone else, I hate that they followed us back to the motel. I wonder if it's dangerous to stay here. I don't think there are a lot of options. I needed to go back to Magnolia Hill this afternoon because I have client meetings tomorrow, but I'm sure Dad's not going to leave until they get to the bottom of Fred's death."

Will nodded in agreement, pulled out his cell phone, and took a picture of the note. While he was snapping the shot, Jillian texted her dad.

—*Are you awake yet?*—

In a few seconds, she got an answer. —*We are. What's up?*—

—*Why don't you come outside?*— she typed with her thumbs. —*Will and I are in the parking lot, and there's something you need to see.*— Jillian leaned back against the orange panel of Will's car. She was barely awake, and she was already tired. The stress of the last two days was catching up with her.

Soon, the door to her parents' room opened, and they came out to the parking lot. Both of their faces were lined with concern, and Jillian hoped for their sakes Fred's murder could be resolved soon.

"What's going on?" her dad asked.

Will walked over to Jillian's father and handed him the paper. "I found this note on my car this morning. I wanted to surprise y'all by picking up some donuts. When I came outside, I found this note on my windshield."

Her father read it and showed it to Jillian's mom. As he handed it back to Will, Jillian saw the paper flutter and realized her dad's hand was shaking.

"I don't like this," he finally said. I don't think it's safe for the two of you to go off investigating." He looked at Will's car, and a hint of a smile formed on his face. "And if you were real detectives, you would know that this is the worst car you could have chosen to be inconspicuous."

Will smiled back. "I know," he said. "But Jillian was tired, and I was trying to make things easier for her. I guess it didn't work."

Jillian reached out and put her arm around his waist. "Don't they say it's the thought that counts? Still, I don't think we should take your car if we go anywhere today."

Jillian's mother's voice shook as she spoke. "I don't want you going anyplace that might be dangerous. I cared for Fred, but I'm more worried about you guys getting hurt or worse." She shuddered as she finished her sentence.

"I hoped to talk to Fred's widow this morning," Jillian said, "but I've got to get back to Magnolia Hill for some meetings tomorrow. Is that okay?" She hated to leave them with Fred's killer still loose.

"Of course," her father said. "You've got a business to run, and we never expected the weekend to be any more than a ghost hunt. Your mom and I are going to stay down here for a few more days. I don't want to leave until they figure out what happened to Fred."

"I may be able to come back late on Tuesday. I don't think I have any meetings Wednesday or Thursday."

"I don't know what you can do." Her dad sighed. "I'm not convinced the local police know what to do either, but the OSBI is supposed to take over today. They're more used to investigating murder."

"Not only that," Jillian's mother interrupted, "I don't want you staying here when you might be in danger. You, Allie, and Will go back today. We'll be fine." She ran her hands down each side of her neck. "Or at least I'll be fine when I can get rid of this headache. The mattress seems to be the same age as the furniture."

"Can I get you anything?" Jillian asked.

"No, I always travel with medicine. Stupid migraines," her mom grumbled.

"I'm sure the stress of this isn't helping either," Will said. "Okay, I'd like to stay. I can't imagine leaving the two of you down here with a killer, but I've got to meet some work deadlines, too. Maybe Jillian and I can come back in the middle of the week if the police still don't know what happened." Jillian nodded, and Will continued.

"I feel weird standing out here in the parking lot. If you want me to, I'll show the note and the hoodie to the police officers before we leave. I'm pretty sure they won't approve of what we did."

"You know they won't," Jillian said. "Couldn't we wait a little longer?" she asked hopefully.

"Why don't you leave them with me," her father suggested. "I'll wait until the OSBI gets involved, and then I'll go talk to them and give them everything. If you're coming back, they can ask you questions then, or they can ZOOM you."

"That seems like a good idea," Jillian said.

"I have lots of friends here, and I don't think anything you've found would make you a suspect. I'd worry about the hoodie, but it smells so bad you obviously pulled it out of the trash. Let's get something to eat before we go talk to Fred's wife, Suzanne. It's too early to drop in."

Jillian texted Allie because her friend never got up this early. She promised to bring her back her favorite Halloween donut, a maple glaze, and suggested that Allie get packed up to leave later that afternoon.

Apparently, Allie was already awake because she messaged back that they couldn't leave soon enough for her.

Chapter Twenty-Three

After donuts and coffee, Jillian's father called Suzanne Winkler. "Jilly, she's glad you want to come by. She remembers you exploring down here as a young girl."

Jillian had memories of a curly-headed, fluffy woman wearing a sleeveless cotton dress and white sneakers. Suzanne must have loved to bake because she always provided fresh cookies for Jillian to munch on while she was doing her own archeological investigations. When Jillian wasn't helping Fred or her dad, she searched the trails for arrowheads, and Suzanne believed she would explore better on a full stomach. Even then, Suzanne behaved like a throwback to a simpler time.

When Will, Jillian, and her parents pulled up to Fred and Suzanne's home, the white clapboard house also evoked an earlier period. The house must have been built at least a hundred years ago, but its fresh white paint and yard filled with orange, yellow, and red chrysanthemums were pretty and simple.

Suzanne opened the front door as soon as they pulled onto the drive, and she stepped onto the concrete porch surrounded by a black wrought-iron fence. Her gray-streaked brown hair was still curly, but her long-sleeved shirtwaist dress hung loosely on her like she lost weight and hadn't purchased new clothes. Jillian didn't know why Suzanne was so much thinner. It was too soon to be the grief, and the older woman didn't look like the kind of person to take diet pills. She came down her three steps with open arms, and when she drew close, Jillian could see her red eyes.

"Robert, Molly, Jillian, thank you for coming to see me." She grabbed all of them in a crushing hug.

As she let them go, Jillian's father stumbled, taking a step backward, and wiped his eyes before he spoke. "Suzanne, I'm so sorry. We all are. Fred was a great man, and I can't believe he's gone. Please let us know if there's anything we can do to help."

"Come in," she said. "And introduce me to your friend, Jillian." Her swollen eyes managed a faint twinkle.

"Suzanne, this is my friend Will Anderson. He's a reporter for the *Magnolia Daily*."

Will had taken Jillian's dad's arm when he stumbled, but he let go and shook Suzanne's hand. "I didn't come here for the story, ma'am," Will added quickly. "Jillian was upset, so I drove down here to see if I could help."

"Seems like you must be a pretty close friend." Suzanne chuckled.

"I'm trying." Will ducked his head and blushed. Jillian couldn't believe she used to think Will was arrogant. Now that they had reconnected, she knew he hated to brag.

Fred's widow welcomed them in, and then she headed for the kitchen. "I put on a pot of coffee when you called, and I hope you're hungry. My friends have brought me tons of food, and even though the kids will get in today, we can't possibly eat it before it goes bad."

Jillian knew that Suzanne was doing everything she could to be gracious, and her heart broke for the brave woman. "Thanks for the offer, but please don't go to any trouble."

"Oh, no trouble at all, child," she said. For a second, Suzanne sounded like Penny, Allie's modern grandmother. But the resemblance ended there. Penny's clothes were stylish and vibrant, and her home was a riot of colors. Suzanne and Fred's home décor could be part of the Oklahoma landscape—rust reds, tans, and light blue. Native American artwork, both modern and ancient, decorated the walls. An upright piano sat centered on the far wall. The only music on it seemed to be a hymnal.

An oak whatnot was hung about two-thirds of the way up the wall in the corner of the room. Jillian hadn't seen one in years. She always liked them because no one could bump into something fragile and break it. Several stone pieces from the Mississippian period decorated the Winkler's whatnot.

Suzanne returned to the room with a tray filled with a percolator coffee pot, teacups and saucers, and the coffee trimmings. She set it on a low table in front of the couch and love seat, and she headed back toward the kitchen.

"Hang on," she said. "I've got to get one more thing." She disappeared back into the kitchen. Soon, she returned with an old-fashioned serving plate heaping with meats, cheeses, cookies, and crackers. "Here you go."

All the place settings matched, and Jillian wished that more people went to that much trouble when they entertained their friends. In an age of Styrofoam cups and paper plates, even Suzanne's refreshments went back to an earlier time.

"Suzanne, you didn't need to do all that," Jillian's mother said.

"I did," Suzanne disagreed. "The food keeps arriving, but I'm not hungry and have more than I can eat. Please. Sharing it with you will make me feel less guilty."

"Thank you. You're very kind." Jillian walked over to the tray and took a piece of cheddar cheese, a wheat cracker, and a chocolate chip cookie. "I love all the Native American art you have in your house."

Suzanne beamed. "Thanks. We've always loved it. Of course, most of them are either inexpensive originals or copies, but that never mattered to either of us."

"No, they're beautiful." Jillian wanted to say that everything reminded her of Fred, but she was sure Suzanne was experiencing the same emotion, and she didn't want to say something that hurt her. "I can't believe Fred's gone. I'm so sorry," she finally offered.

Suzanne stared out the window. "It doesn't seem real. Every minute, I expect him to walk through the door. You know I haven't cried that much? I feel guilty about it, but I just can't believe he's really gone. I know it will all hit at some point, probably when the kids get here." Jillian went up to her and gave her a hug.

"Please know that we will do anything you need," Jillian's dad said. "Molly and I are going to stay down here a few days. Jillian's going back today because she's got meetings on Monday and Tuesday. You know she's a financial planner now." Her father sounded proud.

"But I'm coming back late Tuesday or Wednesday

morning," Jillian assured Suzanne. "I promise we'll figure out who did this to Fred."

Suzanne took a deep breath. "You folks are a real blessing. I know I should tell you to leave it to the police, but they don't seem to have any ideas. Maybe the OSBI will have a better idea of where to begin."

"Do you feel up to answering a few questions?"

"Jillian, I don't feel anything. Maybe I can help you more now than when it all hits."

"Was anybody angry at Fred?" Jillian sat down on a wooden chair with a quilted tan cushion and set her coffee on a rough wood coffee table.

Suzanne shook her head. "When I can stand to think about it, I've been asking myself that same question over and over. I can't think of anything serious." Suzanne paused like she wasn't sure she wanted to continue. Finally, she took a deep breath. "I know that Marlene was angry that he wasn't interested in her."

Jillian was amazed. "You knew about that?"

"Child, Fred told me everything. We were best friends. Yes, I've known for a while that Marlene has tried to catch his eye. He always laughed about it."

"Did she know he was laughing at her?" Will asked.

"I hope not. That would be hateful. But I know he made it clear to her that he wasn't interested. Still, I can't imagine Marlene hurting anyone. I've known her for at least thirty years."

"Was anyone else angry with Fred?"

"I know a few of the private collectors wanted changes to the exhibit tour. They wanted showings in their hometowns, or they wanted the tour longer or shorter. Still, I can't imagine how any of that would lead to one of them killing him."

"Why did they want the tour shorter?" Jillian asked.

"They thought there was a higher possibility that something would be stolen, but Fred promised them he hired plenty of extra security and took precautions."

Jillian and her dad exchanged glances. "Did the police tell you how Fred died?" her father asked.

"Yes. They told me someone hit him on the head," she said softly.

"Did they tell you that the weapon was a Spiro artifact?"

Suzanne turned pale and slumped into her chair, catching herself on the armrests. "Fred was killed by an artifact? I can't believe that. How did the killer get their hands on it?"

"I think it must have been someone with access to the collection. It was cordoned off when we stopped in yesterday," Jillian's dad said. "I'll look at it as soon as the police will let me. Something from the collection should be missing. How else would the killer have gotten a hold of an ancient bowl?"

"I don't know," Suzanne whispered. "Maybe it was Marlene, or maybe it was one of the new security guards. I'm overwhelmed right now, and things seem to roll right over my head."

"We're so sorry," Jillian's mom said. She looked over at her husband. "Robert, I think we should let Suzanne rest now. I'm afraid we're stressing her. We'll check in on you tomorrow if that's okay."

"I'd love that," Suzanne said. "And Jillian, I was thrilled to see you again, even for this awful reason. Will, it was nice to meet you, too."

"I'm sure I'll see you later in the week," Will promised. "I'm going to ride down with Jillian when she comes back. "If she's going to poke around where she shouldn't, I'm not going to let her do it alone."

Chapter Twenty-Four

After they left Suzanne's house, Will, Jillian, and her parents drove back to the motel. Knowing she needed to get on the road soon, Jillian gave her mom and dad big hugs, asking them to be careful. "Please don't do anything to put yourself in danger." Jillian wiped her eyes with the back of her hand.

"Don't cry, Jilly. We'll be careful," her dad promised. "You don't need to come back down. You're probably safer in Magnolia Hill, and I know you don't have any time."

"I'll see how the next couple of days go." Jillian didn't want to argue with him right before she left. She knew she would be back in two days, but it would be easier to leave now if they didn't talk about it.

Will then gave Jillian's mother and father warm embraces. Jillian's dad winked at her over Will's shoulder. Jillian knew her folks hoped that her relationship with Will would get more serious. She was glad everyone got along. Too many families fractured when new relationships changed the dynamics. Even though she and Will had only been dating since the 4th of July, she couldn't imagine her long future without him.

Since they each brought a vehicle, they also gave each other a hug, and Will hopped into his car, closing the door with a mighty squeak. He tapped his squawking horn as he drove his car of many colors out of the lot.

Jillian heard a noise coming from the second floor and saw Allie bringing their cases outside. She ran upstairs to help, and soon, their bags filled the back seat of her truck. They both hugged her mom and dad again and were on the road to Magnolia Hill behind Will.

Jillian and Allie were quiet for several minutes. Allie pulled out a sketch pad while Jillian kept rolling the events of the weekend around in her head. Finally, she spoke. "This weekend didn't turn out like I thought. I was sure we'd have fun hunting a ghost, and instead, I dragged you into a murder investigation."

"It's okay." Allie put down her colored pencils. Jillian glanced at the reds, oranges, and yellows of an impressionistic landscape forming on the sketch pad.

"You're so talented."

"I'm better with colored pencils than I am with crime tape. I'm sorry I didn't help you more. You aren't mad at me, are you?"

Jillian glanced over at Allie, whose big blue eyes were filled with tears.

"Of course, I'm not mad. I'm just sorry I scared you so badly."

"Well, you didn't cause it," Allie corrected. "And I don't want you to think I don't have your back. You know I always do."

"I'm lucky to have you as a best friend," Jilly said.

"Me, too," Allie agreed. "I freaked when I saw Fred's body, and I don't think y'all should be nosing around. Leave the investigation to the police."

"Does this mean you don't want to come back with Will and me Wednesday evening?" Jillian teased.

Allie picked up an orange pencil. "I absolutely do not want to come back here to look for a killer," she said. "Unless you need me," she added after a long pause. "Jeepers, are you going to do that?"

"Probably, but I didn't expect you to join us," Jillian said. "You know, Will's going to come with me."

"I wish he could talk some sense into you, but I think he likes snooping around as much as you do."

"I'm pretty sure he does. And we make a good team."

Allie's mouth finally curved into a huge smile. "That you do," she agreed. "Just try to be careful. Ace and I would miss you both if something happened. And how would we double date?"

"A valid concern," Jillian said. "I promise we'll be careful. Don't forget we've already found several clues. I'm sure Todd is involved. Why else would he have a hoodie with fluorescent paint in the trash?"

"I don't know, but I think you should give it to the police." Allie added some yellow trees to a hill.

"We will, and Dad might tomorrow. Still, I'd like to talk to Todd again before we do. I know how it looks, but I'm not sure he's the murderer."

"And how many murderers do you know?"

"Well, at least one. And who knows how many more?" Jillian tried to make the reminder of her discovery over the summer with a straight face, but a smile tugged the corners of her mouth. "I want to talk to him again, and then I'll turn in the hoodie."

"Someone knows what you two are doing, and they don't like it," Allie reminded her.

"True," Jillian admitted. "No doubt they recognized Will's car."

"Yes, because they left a note on it."

Jillian thought about all the potential suspects she had met over the weekend. "Hey, would you mind writing down a list of names for me?" she asked.

"No problem," Allie said, turning her spiral pad to a new page and digging around in her colored pencils. "I think I'll write it in red for murder."

"Only you would think of that, but I'm glad you're in the spirit of the thing." Jillian smiled at her friend. "Okay, so the killer could be anyone working with the Spiro exhibit. That would even include the extra guards they hired."

"And don't forget Marlene," Allie offered.

"Poor Marlene. Maybe poor Fred. I'm sure he hated to tell her that he wasn't interested. I don't understand how she could know Fred and Suzanne and still think he might be attracted to her."

"Maybe she's lonely. An archeologist who goes home every day to a screaming husband, a cat, and a crock pot meal. From everything you've said, Fred was a great guy. Sounds like he'd be easy to have a crush on," Allie reminded.

"I never thought of him that way. Remember, he reminded me of Einstein."

"He was your father's friend. Of course, you weren't interested in him. And you saw Marlene. She wasn't a real looker herself."

"Don't say that," Jillian objected.

"You know I'm right. I feel bad for Marlene, but I still think she might have killed Fred. Maybe she poured out her heart to him, and he rejected her. She might have grabbed any nearby item and followed him outside when he left. Maybe the artifact was already on her desk, and she was getting it ready to display."

"Maybe," Jillian agreed. "But I still think that's odd. Why would she have used an ancient relic as a weapon? I'm sure she could have grabbed another heavy item from her desk."

"Like what? I was in the Visitor's Center, and I didn't see anything heavy."

"I didn't either," Jillian agreed. "But I still think it's weird. And why was he in the woods? It feels like someone lured him out of sight and killed him."

"Okay, then, who else do I put on the list?"

"Todd seems more likely to me, although I can't figure out how he could have stolen a bowl from the exhibit."

"Maybe he already owned one," offered Allie. She started sketching the murder weapon with her red pencil on the same sheet where she was writing the names. "Wasn't he obsessed with Spiro? At the Center, I read that artifacts were all over the world. Maybe he saved up and bought one."

"Maybe, but like Marlene, I'm surprised he'd risk hurting the artifact by hitting Fred with it. And even if Fred caught him pretending to be a ghost, that doesn't seem like a great reason to kill him," Jillian said.

"Maybe Fred caught him before and threatened to have him arrested. Come on, Jillian. You're the one who reads the mysteries. You know people kill each other for stupid reasons."

Jillian paused for a minute before she answered. "I guess. I have one more name I don't want to add. You don't think Suzanne could have murdered Fred, do you?"

"No. What makes you say that?" Allie asked.

"Maybe Marlene and Fred actually had a thing

going on," Jillian suggested. "Remember, the only two people who told us that Fred wouldn't have dated Marlene are Todd and Suzanne. Todd wouldn't have been close enough to the situation to know the truth. And Suzanne wouldn't tell us the truth if she killed her husband. Still, I can't imagine her killing Fred. She's been kind to me her whole life. She's so distraught that even though I think we shouldn't completely ignore her, I don't want to focus on her, either." The conversation made the drive go by quickly, and Jillian was surprised to see that she was almost back to the interstate.

"Hey, Jilly, talking about murder is making me hungry. Isn't there a fast food restaurant at the next exit?" Allie asked hopefully.

"There is. I could go for a snack, too. We've still got a long drive back to Magnolia Hill."

Chapter Twenty-Five

The next morning, as Jillian was driving to the barn to feed Agatha in the soft autumn light, the problems in Spiro seemed a million miles away. The air was cool, and Jillian smelled faint reminders of a bonfire.

Although she was still anxious to discover who killed Fred, she was glad to be away from the stress for a couple of days. Fear and guilt flashed through her mind as she thought of her parents still down there, but she knew they were cautious and capable.

She walked down the alley that led to Agatha's run and called out her name. When Agatha heard Jillian's voice, she let out a loud nicker. Other horses did, as well. Jillian didn't know if she was popular with people, but she knew she was a rock star with her four-legged friends. She offered quiet pets and nose rubs as she walked by them. She didn't dare speak too loudly, or Agatha would hear. When she got to Agatha's run, the mare's pinned ears showed that she had seen Jillian's infidelity and was none too pleased.

"Oh, Agatha, don't be silly. You know I love you the most," she told the mare. At Jillian's words, Agatha's ears shot forward. She dropped her head and uttered a deep sigh. "Sometimes, I think you speak English." Jillian laughed.

Agatha rubbed her head up and down against the

fence post. Maybe she was agreeing, and maybe she was scratching a late-season fly. Jillian couldn't wait until the first freeze. The cold snaps wouldn't last long at first, but they would kill off most of the biting insects that still plagued the horses and their owners working outdoors.

Jillian pulled some treats out of the pocket of her jeans and fed a couple of them to Agatha. Mister noticed the treats, walked over, and let out a small, polite nicker.

"Of course," Jillian responded. "Here you go, buddy." The black and white paint took the treats as Agatha pinned her ears again.

"Settle down," Jillian reminded her, but she still grabbed another treat for the mare.

At the end of Agatha's run, Jillian was shocked to see a large hole. "That's where you were digging before I left for Spiro," she told the horse.

Agatha nodded her head up and down, or maybe she was chewing.

"Why are you digging a hole in your run?"

Agatha looked away, ignoring both Jillian and Mister.

"Are you trying to dig something up or bury something?" Jillian asked the mare. "Silly dogs act like that, not horses. You're supposed to be too refined to dig in the dirt."

Agatha stared at Jillian, gave a nicker, went back to her hole, and started digging again with her hoof.

"Stop, sweet girl. I don't want you to create something dangerous. You could break your own leg if you stepped into that hole."

Agatha glared at Jillian and gave her tail an angry swish. A fly on her side flew off.

"I'll call the barn manager and try to get some dirt.

Maybe she'll even fill the hole for us. If not, I'll get it as soon as I can. Love you. I'll see you this evening or tomorrow."

Agatha nickered and then went back to digging.

As Jillian drove home, she wondered why Agatha started excavating her run. In cold or stormy weather, when she put her up in a stall, Agatha pawed because she wanted out, but she never did that in her indoor-outdoor run. Of course, she liked her pasture better, but she never appeared depressed or distressed beside Mister.

After a quick call to the barn manager, she pulled into the bank on her way to work. If she was heading back to Spiro later in the week, she needed more cash.

When she entered the one-story stucco building, she grabbed a Styrofoam cup of coffee and a chocolate cake donut with orange sprinkles. Her friend and vice-president of Sooner Bank, Jennifer Browne, waved her into her office. Jennifer's green suit accented her red hair, and her metallic orange and green lapel pin of a pumpkin on a vine kept the autumn spirit. Jillian loved her friend's pins even though she couldn't wear jewelry that large.

She set her cup of coffee on the edge of Jennifer's desk, so she wouldn't drop the donut. The normally convenient coffee table was fully decorated with a lighted haunted house surrounded by miniature candy bars.

"I saw you on the news," Jennifer said instead of a more conventional greeting.

"Oh, no. Did they play the video here?" Jillian slumped in her chair.

"You got caught in the shot. They aired it on the local stations because of Fred Winkler's connection to the university. I can't believe someone killed him. He was a friend of your father's, wasn't he?"

"Yes, but I barely saw him when he was here. Most of my memories are from his work at Spiro, even before he got the job as director. Such a nice guy." Jillian wondered how much the local media knew. "Did the news release information about the murder weapon?"

"Not that I've heard," Jennifer said. "You know how fast the news moves on. I suspect they won't do another story until the murderer has been caught. Do you know how he died?" Jennifer always loved a good story.

"The police found something." Jillian didn't want to admit that she also found the murder weapon, and she justified her omission because nothing was confirmed yet. "I don't know exactly what it was, and I suspect they are trying to keep that information quiet until they have someone in custody."

"I can't believe you've gotten tangled up in two murders this year," Jennifer said.

"At least only one of them was in Magnolia Hill," Jillian defended. "In fact, I'm going back to Spiro later this week after I have a couple of meetings. I'm getting cash now because my schedule will get worse before it gets better."

"If you hear anything interesting, please let me know." Jennifer dropped her voice even though her office door was closed. "I'm assuming you're going back down to try to figure out who killed Fred," she continued.

"Mom and Dad are still there, and I don't want them looking around by themselves. Will's going to drive down with me, and I'll be glad to have his company."

"Not to mention his size. You'll be safer."

"That, too," Jillian agreed.

"And his rugged good looks," Jennifer continued. "I'm so glad you guys are finally dating. I think you're perfect for each other."

Jillian felt her face heat, and she looked down like she was studying the ceramic haunted house. "It's still early," she said. "But we have a lot of fun together, and I do like having backup if I want to go exploring."

"Be safe," Jennifer cautioned. "If you know more than you're telling me, and I suspect you do..."

Jillian tried to interrupt her, but Jennifer waved her hand. "Please. I've known you forever. You can do many things, but you can't lie to save your life. As I was saying," she continued, giving Jillian a stern look, "someone has killed before. They won't hesitate to do it again."

Chapter Twenty-Six

As Jillian left the bank, she waved at the security guard outside the door. Jennifer's warning replayed in her head. She should call her parents to check on them and remind them to be careful. As she started to dial, her phone rang, and Allie's face popped up on her truck's hands-free display. She tapped the answer button.

"Hey, friend, did you get enough sleep last night?"

"Don't make fun. I've been up for hours. I went to my studio and worked on my commission, which is due by the middle of November. It's too big for my garage, and I'd rather work on a second batch of pumpkins for the nursing home tonight when I can be home."

"I don't blame you," Jillian agreed. "You're doing so well. More commission work and less fence painting."

"I am," Allie said proudly. "But the real test will be in the spring. Right now, most people aren't thinking about outside projects. Once it's April and May, they will want their yards looking nice for the summer. If I can keep busy with commission work, then I'll know my income focus is changing. But that's not why I called you."

"What's up?" Jillian asked.

"When I went to the gallery this morning, Don White came rushing up to me. He saw us on the news."

Jillian groaned. "I know. Jennifer at the bank saw

us, too. I guess we should assume that the entire world knows we found the body."

"He said he saw us, and then he started sobbing and hugging me. He told me he couldn't believe someone had killed his friend. I didn't know what to do, so I hugged him back."

"That's so sad," Jillian said. "Don, Fred, and my dad were close. I didn't know Don as well as Fred, but I'm sure he's devastated."

"Once he pulled himself together a little bit, he wanted to talk about what had been happening at the site. He really focused on Todd and his podcasts."

"That seems odd. Why?"

"He said he's known him for years. Wait—that's not quite right. He claimed Todd had bugged him for years."

"So he thinks Todd's annoying?"

"He doesn't like him at all. He said that Todd exaggerates all his stories. Don thinks he does it to help his podcasts make more money. Until all of this happened, I didn't know you could make a living as a podcaster."

Jillian noticed the security guard looking at her as she sat in her truck. She offered him a cheery smile and another wave. She didn't want him to think she was doing anything shady.

"I didn't either," she admitted. "I like to listen to them, especially the true crime ones, but I never thought about them as someone's full-time job. Will knows more about them than I do, and he told me that good podcasters can get sponsors and sell merch. You can make a lot of money if you're good and get a little lucky. I wonder if Todd creates his own luck."

"Don seems to think so. He believes Todd was more

sensational than factual, and he thinks that Todd made up the ghost to help his ratings."

"That would tie to the blue paint on Todd's hoodie."

"Right. Don thinks that Fred probably caught Todd pretending to be a ghost and that Todd killed him to keep his behavior a secret."

Jillian paused before she spoke. "That still seems extreme to me. I know we talked about Todd before your conversation with Don, but I still think it's not much of a motive. Would you really kill someone over lowering your T-shirt and hat sales?"

"I asked Don the same thing. He said that for the amount of money Todd was making, it was more than enough motive."

Jillian wondered why Don was so interested in blaming Todd. Did he know about the Marlene incident and want to protect Suzanne? "It seems like Don is providing us with a lot of information about Todd. How does he know that the podcast merchandise is making a lot of money?"

"Don said he went to Spiro about a month ago to help with the traveling display. He saw Todd pull into the parking lot driving a brand-new sports car. Jilly, he told me he'd seen cars like that sell for $75,000. Can you imagine?"

"That's a lot of money," Jillian agreed. "But I've seen plenty of vehicles sell for that or more. Still, it's expensive for a young podcaster. I wonder how he got the money?" Jillian started her truck, so she could run her air conditioning. Even though it was October, the weather was still almost hot in the middle of the day.

"With $75,000, I wouldn't buy a fancy sports car," Allie insisted. "I'd try to buy my condo. I bet with that down payment, my landlord would sell it to me. She's said many times she's tired of the hassles of dealing with renters."

"Do you bother her?" Jillian teased.

"No, but some of her other tenants do," Allie said.

"Will and I didn't see a sports car on the drive when we drove by Todd's place, and he certainly wasn't driving a car that expensive when we met with him."

"Did he have a garage?" Allie asked.

"He did. He must have parked it inside. I know I would. He would have to sell a lot of T-shirts and hats to earn that much money. I wonder if he's using his podcast to hide an illegal source of funds."

"Like drugs?"

"Maybe drugs. Maybe something else. He might have used the money to buy the car."

"I wouldn't want a car that cost that much," Allie insisted. "Jillian, I'm not trying to throw you and Will under the bus, but I think your parents need to give Todd's hoodie to the police."

"That will look great," Jillian said, unable to keep the sarcasm from her voice.

"I know. But if Don's right and Todd thought that Fred was about to expose his cash cow, then Todd is probably the killer."

"Right. And we did see someone with blue paint running away. I was going to call Dad right before you called me. Maybe he can come up with a story that doesn't make us look like we're meddling."

"If the police don't know where to turn, then Todd isn't a suspect," Allie said. "You've done more than they have. You've found literally everything. Fred, the bowl, and the sweatshirt. Then, he would have gotten away with it. Don's distraught that something could happen to your dad."

"Did you tell him they were down there?" Jillian asked.

"No, I didn't have to. He said that the story is all over the department. Everyone knows that Molly and Bob Bradford are in Spiro trying to find Fred's killer."

"I don't like that," Jillian said grimly. "I'll call them the minute I get off the phone with you. The police may be upset with us, but you're right. We've helped them out a lot with this."

"Yes, we have. Anyway, I need to get some lunch and go back to the studio. Got time to grab a sandwich?"

At the mention of lunch, Jillian's stomach growled. She ignored it, knowing that her schedule would get in the way. "I wish, but I've got two client meetings this afternoon, and then I have to fill a hole. Agatha's started pawing her run, and she's dug a substantial pit."

"That's weird. Has she ever done that before?"

"Never. I need to fill it before she manages to stumble into it."

"Good luck."

"And Allie, if you see Don again, please tell him thanks. The faster the police can get Fred's killer behind bars, the safer we'll all be."

Chapter Twenty-Seven

Jillian drove away from the bank, offering the guard a final cheery smile and wave. He gave a small, bemused wave back. She pulled into a parking space in front of her office. Even though the summer heat broke earlier in the month, she liked to be able to park in front of her door rather than halfway down the block.

Katherine was coming in later that day, so Jillian reviewed the client packet her assistant created the day before. As she checked for all the documents, she was glad she had been able to reach her parents. Her father promised to take the hoodie to the police. When she asked him what he was going to say, he told her not to worry. Fortunately, his many friends in Spiro could vouch that he wasn't a murderer.

The new client arrived ten minutes early, and Jillian immediately felt a chill in the room. The young woman, named Morti, was wearing a black tunic with a sheer black skirt, black hose, and black combat boots, and a spiderweb tattoo started on the back of her left hand and ran up her arm. Jillian also thought she recognized her perfume. Was it Poison? Never mind, she asked her what she could do to help.

"I'm trying to update my investments, but I'm getting conflicting views," Morti said.

"Financial advisers can have quite different

opinions about what is best for your portfolio," Jillian explained. She didn't like to be critical unless she believed the other adviser was deliberately exploiting the client.

"Oh, it's not my financial adviser," the woman said. "I don't have one."

Jillian paused before she continued. "Well, you should also be careful taking advice from friends, too," she cautioned. "Even if they mean well, they may have different needs or goals than you have."

"I never talk to my friends about investments."

Jillian was confused and slightly unsettled. "Okay." She knew the word stretched out longer than it should. "Do you mind telling me who you're asking?"

The woman across the table smiled at something only she could see. "Well, my spirit guides, of course."

Jillian couldn't help but glance across the table. She saw nothing. "Of course."

The woman continued. "One guide is telling me to buy large cap, and one guide is telling me to buy international. A third guide wants me to buy a specific stock." She mentioned the name of a company in the news recently. "What do you think I should do?"

Jillian resisted the urge to ask her to quit consulting spirits about her portfolio. "Well, first, we would need to look at the goals you have for your money. Then, we'd look at how much risk you want to take and your current portfolio holdings. I couldn't give you advice until I knew that."

The woman offered a thin, musical laugh that made the hair on the back of Jillian's neck stand up. "That's silly. I only want to own what is making the most money. Then, I want you to sell it when it slows down and buy me whatever is making the most money then."

"I wish I could do that," Jillian said. "We would all make a huge profit. Unfortunately, investing in the market doesn't work like that. We use your risk tolerance and diversification to help you meet your goals. Of course, I follow economic and market news, and that can help guide some decisions, but I can't tell you what will make the most money. No one can do that."

"No one who is mortal, you mean," the woman snapped. Her eyes flashed. "Fine, I'll go home and consult Seraphina and do what she says."

"Who is Seraphina?"

"My familiar, my cat, of course," the woman huffed. "I'm sorry I wasted your time. Good day."

She swished out of the conference room, and the door closed behind her on its own.

"Geez," Jillian said to herself. The hairs on her arm were standing straight up, and she was freezing cold. "I hope her cat is better at predicting the market than Edgar." She opened the conference door, went into the lobby, and looked outside to see where Morti had gone. The woman was walking up the street. Jillian noticed a broom leaning against the wall of another building, and she closed the door before Morti reached it. She didn't want to know.

She checked her watch, discovered she had almost an hour before her next meeting, and made herself an individual cup of coffee. She needed to warm up, and she desperately hoped the next client would be sane.

Chapter Twenty-Eight

After changing into barn clothes and boots that she had brought with her, Jillian left her office after work to go directly to the stables. As she walked to her truck, she couldn't help but check for the broom. It was gone, but surely a shop owner had taken it back inside. On her way to the barn, she thought back to her second meeting that afternoon. Fortunately, it was more normal than the first meeting.

This client was signing the paperwork to open an IRA and roll over a 401(k) from a previous employee. He was happy to look at his risk tolerance and asset allocation, and he didn't want to consult his cat with her recommendations. His only confusion concerned the mandatory money laundering questions, especially those that asked how the money was earned and whether the bank accounts were foreign or housed within the United States.

She saw his point. If someone were going to launder money, why would they tell the truth about how they obtained it? If they were terrorists, why would they be honest about that? She knew the required information placed her client on the record, and she frequently answered questions like the new client's. Nearly always, everything went smoothly.

One time, a client's questions and responses got her

attention. He seemed angry that she was asking him where his money came from. She tried to explain that the questions were standard, and she worked in some additional information through a casual conversation. Finally, when he mentioned he worked in IT security, she realized he wasn't a crook. He was only obsessed with his privacy. She wondered how often her new client application forms caught illegal behavior. She hoped they did, but she wasn't sure.

When she got to the barn, she was relieved to see that the manager had filled the hole with dirt and provided an additional pile for her to add. She grabbed her shovel, tamped down the existing dirt in the hole as best she could, and added more on top. She had been hot in her truck, but working in the sun was even worse. It was hard to get into the Halloween spirit when it was ninety degrees, but she hoped Agatha's fun lights would help. From the end of the run, her handiwork from a few days earlier was obvious. Poor Fred had been alive when she hung the lights. She shook her head. Maybe they were close to proving that Todd was the killer.

Finally finished, she gave Agatha a hug around her large neck, and the horse rested her head on top of Jillian's cap. "Silly girl, don't dig another hole, okay?"

Agatha rubbed her head side to side on top of Jillian's cap. Was she saying no, or did her chin itch? Jillian knew that sometimes she gave the horse credit she didn't deserve, but she believed Agatha was close to communicating with her. She gave a laugh, and Agatha moved away. She needed to be careful, or she'd soon be as crazy as the woman who asked her cat for investment advice.

"Bye, sweetheart! I'll try to see you tomorrow. If I

can't, I'll only be gone for a few days. Mister's mom will feed you, so don't panic.

At the word "feed," Agatha sniffed her bowl, licked the black plastic, and focused sad eyes on Jillian. Jillian gave her a final couple of cookies, wrapped her arms around her neck again, and left. She was dirty, sweaty, and furry, and she couldn't wait to get home to a shower before she made dinner plans.

Her father called as she drove home. "You are lucky that I've got great connections in Spiro."

"Oh, geez, what did the police say?"

"Apparently, it's illegal to go dumpster diving on private property. Technically, you were trespassing, but the police are going to let it go. You're also lucky that when you talked to law enforcement after you found Fred's body, you mentioned seeing someone wearing a hoodie with fluorescent paint. Your story was consistent. However, they would like for you to consent to a DNA swab when you come back."

"My DNA will be on the hoodie because I touched it," Jillian reminded him.

"Yes, but not on the inside. You didn't try it on, did you?" her father asked.

"That stinky thing? No way, and we bagged it as quickly as we could."

"The police don't think it's yours, so you shouldn't have any issues. In fact, I wouldn't be surprised if they arrested Todd tonight or tomorrow. I talked to the local officers, and they want to solve the case before the OSBI gets involved. You know how tensions between local and state can run."

"I do." Jillian recalled several conversations with Will. "The sooner anyone can arrest Fred's killer, the happier I will be. I'll come down either way to provide the DNA sample, and I'm sure Will would be willing to do the same thing. We'll see you late tomorrow."

"Okay, I'll reserve a couple of hotel rooms for you guys."

"Thanks, Dad. I'll talk to Will about the DNA when we go to dinner tonight."

After she got home, she fed Edgar. His yowling and jumping from place to place weren't going to allow her to do anything else first. As she put down his bowl of wet food, she petted his back, and he arched it under the weight of her palm. "Edgar, do you want to help me select investments?" Edgar ignored her and focused on devouring his fishy feast. "That's what I thought. If you ever change your mind, let me know." He never raised his head from his bowl.

After she showered and changed into a pair of ankle-length jeans, a yellow T-shirt, and a sunflower scarf kimono, she texted Will and asked when he wanted to have dinner. He messaged back that he would be done in half an hour. Where did she want to go? Jillian wanted a good cup of coffee as badly as she wanted food.

—*Kandace's?*—

Will replied with a thumbs up.

Jillian decided to drive to Kandace's early, so she would have some time to talk to her friend because she watched the news and would want the details of what happened.

Chapter Twenty-Nine

Jillian opened the door to Bits, Bytes, and Brews, and the heavenly scent of ground and brewed coffee, along with baking pastries wrapped around her. She found a spot and organized her bag. Kandace rolled over to the table.

"It's good to see you, friend. Are you here for coffee or dinner?"

"Both. Will's going to join me, but I would love a mug of peaberry coffee before he gets here."

"I'll get it for you. Do you have time to talk, or do you need to work?" Kandace asked.

"I have time. I was hoping you'd be free. I have a couple of things I wanted to ask you about."

"I'll bet. I'll be right back with the coffee."

Jillian loved the chrome and polished tile coffee shop. Beside the cash register was the day's special written on a chalkboard. The "screaming zombie," served hot or iced, featured coffee flavored with dark chocolate, cayenne, and cherry syrup. Whipped cream sprinkled with more cayenne topped either drink. Jillian liked spice, but today, she needed regular coffee.

Soon, Kandace returned with two cups. Jillian moved one of the chairs, and Kandace rolled up to the table. She wasted no time getting to her question.

"Did you and Allie really find the body?" she asked.

"We did," said Jillian. "And I want to ask you some questions about it, but I have a more important concern."

Kandace quirked her eyebrow. "Okay, you go first."

"How's Bud?" Jillian asked with a big smile.

Kandace looked down, her shoulder-length brown hair falling forward. Finally, she looked back up at Jillian, and her face was bright red. "I told Bud I wanted us to have some time to get acquainted. I guess he told Gayle?"

"Who told Allie, who told me not to tell anyone. And I haven't other than you right now," Jillian said. "But after all the awful things that happened last weekend, I need to hear some good news."

"Okay, fine, but please try to keep it quiet. I'm sure it will be everywhere soon enough. After all, this is a small town."

"I won't talk to anyone else. I haven't even told Will yet. But I'm curious, and I want to know if I should be happy for you."

Kandace's face lit with the brightest smile Jillian had ever seen. "Yes, you can be happy for me. Bud is a great guy, and he's so interested in everything I tell him. We even have some similar hobbies. We both love music, books, and fantasy-based television, movies, and games."

"That's so cool." Jillian bent down to give her friend a big hug. "I'm more than happy—I'm thrilled for you. Will and I would love to double date with you anytime you want."

"That would be fun. And I think we should include Allie and Ace. You know, Allie likes to work on her social media here, and even though she hasn't said anything, her smile has brightened every time she sees me. I had a feeling she knew."

"We're all happy for you, but we will give you and Bud all the time you need."

"Thanks, friend. Now, we need to talk about you rather than my love life. So, you and Allie really found the body? I'm sorry."

"Me, too. It was awful, and it totally freaked Allie out. I'm not sure she will ever take a weekend trip with me again."

Kandace shook her head in agreement. "I can't blame her for that. You have a weird talent for getting caught up in murder investigations. Can you share anything?"

Jillian knew it wasn't fair for her to ask for information and then not provide anything in return, but she was already in enough trouble with the police in Spiro. "I'm so sorry, Kandace. I can't get ahead of the authorities, but I think the police may arrest the killer soon."

"Well, everybody's talking about the death of Fred Winkler. He was a local celebrity, and folks are sad and shaken about what happened, even if it wasn't here."

"I know. It's the first question everybody asks me," Jillian said.

"Last night, Don White's teaching assistant, Harvey, came by for a cup of coffee and a pumpkin cinnamon roll," Kandace said. "He told me how great a mentor Fred had been to him. He participated in several digs during the Spiro summer programs, where Fred taught him hands-on skills. He explained that seeing the real artifacts showed him the importance of creating 3-D renderings for his students."

"He makes 3-D copies of Spiro artifacts?"

"He does. He uses them in the undergraduate classes he teaches. He told me it would be impossible to show many students the real artifacts because they might be damaged. Some of his lower-level classes have over fifty enrolled. However, 3-D copies are so similar to the originals that they provide a good substitute. Harvey told me that helping the ancient cultures come to life made it more realistic for his students. Harvey's a nice guy. I think he'll make a great archeologist, himself, someday."

"That's cool," Jillian exclaimed. "I'm surprised the poor quality of the copies doesn't make the artifacts look cartoonish."

"Friend, you are behind the times," Kandace said. "I bet you got one of those cheesy Eiffel Towers at a demonstration."

"How did you know?"

"Because I got one, too. I still have mine. Today's printers are so much more advanced than that. They can print in filament, resin, stone, and even metal. They can also print in high-quality color, or the replicas can be painted after they are created."

Jillian took a sip of her coffee. "I had no idea. So if you viewed the item rather than lifting it, you couldn't tell it from the original?"

"They're so good that some museums are making 3-D replicas of priceless items and storing the originals. According to Harvey, the Arkansas Archeological Survey also has a program to replicate Mississippian-era artifacts. It helps ensure that the original irreplaceable pieces stay safe."

"Wow, that's impressive," Jillian said.

Kandace continued, "Of course, some artifacts replicate more easily than others. Highly textured items are more difficult and expensive to copy. But with many pieces, most people can't tell the difference. And they might think a copy is real even if they held it. There are ways to add weights to the replica while it's being created. The technology is stunning."

"How did you learn all of that?" Jillian asked, impressed with Kandace's knowledge.

"I've been a fan since I got my Eiffel Tower," Kandace admitted. "And I've learned a lot about it from Harvey."

Jillian shook her head. "I know I sound old, but between artificial intelligence and 3-D modeling, think about all the things that students can experience today. The replicas aren't historical, like the real artifacts, but they are certainly more inspiring than pictures in a textbook."

As she finished her coffee, Will came through the door. He gave her a hug and offered Kandace a fist bump. "Ladies, how were your days?"

"Not bad. Just busy," Kandace said.

"My afternoon was less bizarre than my morning." Jillian summarized her concern with asking a cat for financial advice. She was careful never to share client names or identifying information with friends and family, but some stories were too good to keep to herself. Kandace and Will laughed at the encounter.

"I have to admit, I'm glad she doesn't want to be a client. It sounds like she might cast a spell on you if you lost money," Will said.

"Are you done with hauntings?" Kandace asked Will.

"For the next five Halloweens. Still, I want to help Jillian's folks. It's important that Fred's murder be solved."

"Speaking of that," Jillian interrupted, "I promised Dad that you and I would provide DNA samples to the local police. They want to compare it to what they found inside the hoodie."

"Won't comparing DNA take weeks?" Kandace asked.

Jillian shrugged, but Will spoke up. "It might, but there's new technology that can give the police a fast analysis. Rapid DNA testing only takes a few hours."

"So, reality is finally catching up with television," Jillian said. "It always bothered me that law enforcement technology that took weeks to analyze in real life could be solved by television detectives in a few days."

"I agree," Will said. "Rapid DNA is a game changer. It's remarkable how quickly the technicians can get preliminary results."

"I agree with you, Jillian. The world is changing quickly, and if that makes me sound old, so be it," Kandace said. "All right, I'll let you two have some time. Will, what do you want to drink, and what can I get you both to eat?"

In addition to offering fresh ground coffee beans from around the world, extraordinary coffee drinks, and internet access, Kandace also served "bytes," tapas-style snacks and entrees. Jillian thought it was no surprise everyone she knew loved Kandace and Bits, Bytes, and Brews. She grabbed her phone and quickly chose from the QR code menu.

"I'd like the prosciutto and pesto sliders," Jillian said.

"I can get you a P-squared. Will?"

"I'd like mint iced tea with the grilled cheese

triangles and a cream of tomato soup. Do you have any today?"

"I do. That soup's so popular that I've added it to the daily menu. I'll go put in your orders."

"Feel free to come back to the table and visit if you have any free time," Jillian said. "I'm always interested in what you've discovered."

"The only useful conversation I've had was with Harvey. Otherwise, people are horrified both about the crime and that you and Allie have wound up in the middle of it. Again," she said, referring to their adventures over the summer.

"I'm ready for it to be over. I think it might wrap up soon."

"You know something." Kandace shot her an accusing glance.

"I have some suspicions," Jillian admitted. "We'll know tonight or tomorrow if we see it on the news."

Chapter Thirty

Even though Jillian knew that Will would be happy to share their dinner time with Kandace, she also thought he wanted to talk to her about Fred's case. While Kandace was still at the table, she had seen him run his hand through his hair a couple of times, a behavior Jillian had learned meant that he was worried about something.

"Hey, did you have a stressful day? You asked us, but we didn't return the favor."

"You could say that." Will sighed as he ran his hand through his dark hair again.

"Anything you want to talk about?" she asked.

He closed his eyes. "No," then he opened them again. "Wait, I'm not going to make that mistake again. Could we talk about something I'm trying to deal with?"

For a minute, Jillian forgot about Fred, Harvey, and her folks. She was thrilled he wanted to bring her into his confidence. She put her hand on his arm. "Of course, we can. What's going on?"

"You know what I told you about Amber?"

"Yes, is she in trouble?"

"I don't know. Maybe. Remember how Josh's father has been hassling her since he learned we told a few people what happened back in high school."

"You mean people like me?"

"You and a couple of my friends. Once the story was

out, I wanted to clear my name with a few people."

"I still don't understand why he's so freaked out about something in the past."

"In his generation, folks believed that people should pull themselves up by their bootstraps. That kind of thing." Will shook his head. "Anyway, he told her that he'll leave her alone, but she has to promise never to mention Josh's name again. Also, he wants me to run a positive story about a new business venture Josh is starting."

"Who does he think he is? He can't control the press," Jillian said indignantly.

Will chuckled. "I appreciate your concern, but I'm thinking the *Magnolia Daily* is just barely 'the press.' Most of the time, we feature the topics of our local civic group meetings, the grade school lunch menu, and obituaries."

"I know, but it's the idea of the thing," Jillian insisted. "Are you going to do it?"

"I don't know. I want to hear what you think." He leaned back and smiled at her.

Jillian was thrilled he wanted to include her in his decision-making process. She thought for a minute before she responded. "Take a step back from the people involved. Pretend Josh's dad isn't hassling you. Do you think what Josh is doing is interesting? Do you think he will be successful?"

"It's interesting enough," Will admitted. "If his father hadn't told me to run the story, I probably would have covered it anyway. But I'm not sure I'm comfortable with him thinking he can control me."

"Will he stop hassling Amber if you guys do what he wants?"

"I think so. I also know that in Oklahoma, it's legal to tape a conversation if one side knows. My tape recorder on my phone ran during our entire conversation. I could always make a story out of that if he doesn't stop bullying Amber."

The coffee house wasn't overly cold, but Jillian shivered anyway. "He's a dangerous man, and he's power-hungry. Please be careful. I don't want to see you or Amber have an issue with him."

"I don't intend to do anything with my tape, but I like having it," Will said. "Do you think I should run the story?"

"I think you should treat it like any other lead. If you'd run it without his father's threats, then I think you should cover the business. If you wouldn't do a story on it, then don't."

Will's shoulders relaxed as he exhaled. "It's really that easy, isn't it?" he asked. "The history of this thing has gotten into my head. You're right. I'll ignore his dad and do what I want. I'll probably cover it because I would have done it any other time." He leaned across the table and looked her in the eyes. Jillian's heart pounded in her chest. "Did I ever tell you you're smart?" he asked.

"Every once in a while," Jillian said. "But I only help you make the decisions you would have come to on your own. You just might have taken a little longer without me," she teased before she leaned across the table and gave him a quick kiss. She sat up straight when a server brought them their meals.

Chapter Thirty-One

Jillian was home from her dinner with Will before the ten o'clock news, so she plopped down on her brown leather couch, kicked off her shoes, and put her feet up. She pulled off a brown, red, and turquoise Navajo blanket hanging over the couch and covered her feet. Even though the days were still warm, sometimes even hot, the nights were beginning to get cool.

Edgar jumped up, turned three careful circles, and settled on the blanket beside her feet. One green eye and one exposed ear ensured he wouldn't miss anything. Jillian turned on the news and was surprised to see a video of Todd being led away by the Spiro police. Even though the shot was more from the back than the side, his spiky hair made him recognizable. The chyron read, "Podcaster Arrested for Murdering Director of Spiro Archeological Park."

Jillian turned the television up louder to hear the newscaster explain how Todd pretended to be a ghost that first haunted Spiro during the 1920s. The earnest reporter, wearing a polo shirt from her station, went on to describe the hoodie splattered with fluorescent paint. She explained that the police believed Todd killed Fred when the director discovered the fraud. They conjectured that Todd recreated the spirits to increase his podcast's subscribers and monetization.

Jillian looked down at Edgar. "I wonder how they figured all of that out?" she said slyly.

Edgar offered a "Mrrp" in response.

Soon, the news coverage moved on to discuss steps parents should take to protect their children as they went Trick or Treating. That story led into the weather forecast for Halloween, cool and cloudy. The anchors all grinned with glee at the thought of a spooky Halloween, the story of Fred Winkler forgotten.

Jillian turned off her television and considered calling her father. She knew he must be relieved for Todd to be in custody, and they might have gone to bed early. Her ringing phone interrupted her thoughts, and her father's image smiled up from the screen.

"Hi, Dad. I wasn't sure if you and Mom were still up. I saw the story about Todd's arrest on the news. I'm sure you're both relieved he's in custody."

"I am." Her father's voice sounded flat.

"You don't sound pleased," she said. "I know you're still upset about Fred's death, but I was hoping Todd's arrest might give you closure."

"It does," he continued, still measuring his words. "I'm not sure…" he trailed off. "I'm just not sure he's the killer."

"Why not?" Jillian asked with surprise. "Everything points to him."

"I know," her dad said. "And I'm the one who gave the information to the police. That's why I have pause and regrets tonight."

"Did something else happen?"

"Well, you know the old stereotype of the defendant being given one phone call?"

"Yes."

"Todd used one of his limited calls to contact me."

"What?" Jillian sat up straight on her couch, and Edgar gave her a dirty look as he curled back up on the crumpled blanket. "Why did he call you, and how did he have your number?"

"Todd's had my number for years. He's always loved Spiro. He called to ask me to help him. He swore he didn't kill Fred. He promised he knew nothing about the body until he heard you scream."

"So we did see him that night?"

"You did. He admitted to pretending to be the ghost, and he threw away his hoodie after you and Will talked to him. He said he pulled off the scam to bring more attention to the site. He also mentioned that he was concerned about something odd happening with the artifacts."

"Like Fred?"

"Maybe. Remember, Fred never gave me details, but their concern sounded similar. Anyway, Todd didn't have enough time to explain it to me, but he swore he wasn't a murderer."

Jillian took a deep breath. "Dad, I know this has been awful for you and Mom in every way. Still, don't you think a murderer would lie if he wanted your sympathy?"

"Maybe," her dad admitted. "But I'm not sure."

"What are you going to do?"

"I'm going to call Ken Griffen. He's a good criminal attorney in Poteau." Her father gave a deep sigh. "Jillian, I'm the one who has put this man in jail, maybe facing the death penalty if he's found guilty. If there's even a small chance he didn't do it, I need to give him the opportunity to prove it."

"Just be careful if he gets released."

"I don't think the police release people charged with murder. They'll need a better suspect before they let him go."

"Well, I have another client meeting tomorrow morning, and I want to run by the bank and ask Jennifer a question. I think Will and I will be driving down by five or so. Don't wait for us for dinner," she said. "We'll probably grab something to go on our way down."

"You know you don't have to come."

"I know, but you promised that we'd give a DNA sample," she reminded him.

"Oh, that's right. Sorry about that." Edgar curled tight in a ball on the blanket and began to snore softly.

"No problem. But remember, Dad, I don't think you're right, but if you are, the real murderer is still free. He or she isn't going to appreciate your continuing to stay involved." Jennifer's words echoed again in Jillian's head.

"I know. Your mom and I talked about it. I know I can trust Ken, so I'm going to call him tomorrow morning. I'm not going to tell anyone else that I've paid for the attorney."

"Dad, you could call the attorney without paying the bill," Jillian chided.

"I'll work out the payment later. I don't think Todd has a lot of money. Anyhow, I appreciate your concern. I promise we'll be cautious."

"Don't trust anyone, not even Suzanne," Jillian said.

"I know. We can be supportive and kind without telling her everything we're thinking."

"Okay. Good night. Love you and Mom."

"Love you more. And remember that if we're in

danger, you are, too. Of course, we can explain your return to Spiro as the need for your DNA, but that will only give you cover for a day. You need to be careful."

Chapter Thirty-Two

Jillian woke up early the next morning, knowing she probably had more work than time. Edgar yawned and stretched briefly as she crawled out of bed, but he soon curled into a little black ball on her pillow. His morning wasn't going to start this early.

She threw on some casual clothes, drove to the barn, and pulled up to the far end of Agatha's run. The mare raised her head in surprise when she saw Jillian in her truck. Fortunately for both horses, she always kept a bag of treats in her center console. Agatha walked toward Jillian's truck, and Mister walked down his run, as well, both horses looking hopeful.

Jillian stepped outside her truck and examined the hole she filled the day before. It wasn't as deep, but Agatha had certainly removed some of the dirt again.

"Pretty girl, what are you doing?"

Agatha ignored the question, stretching her neck to get her head as close to Jillian as possible. Jillian gave treats to both horses and looked again at the hole. Almost on cue, Agatha walked over and began to dig again.

"Are you trying to give me a message?" Jillian asked, hoping no one could overhear her.

Agatha nodded her head up and down, or maybe she was just chewing her cookie.

"Are you trying to dig something up?"

Agatha nodded or chewed again. Mister munched away, having no interest in the conversation, but he definitely wanted another cookie, so he rubbed his nose on Jillian's arm.

"Okay, boy, here's one more cookie for you, and Agatha, you get one more, as well. Please stop digging. I don't have a lot of time today, so I'll get help filling the hole again. At least we have some extra dirt. I'll be gone a couple more days this week, but you're in good hands. I'll see you as soon as I get back. I'll have Halloween treats for you," she promised.

Agatha nickered and dropped her head. Sometimes, Jillian wondered what she understood. Like many animals, her mare knew a few words, like "treat," but surely she couldn't hold an entire conversation, could she?

Jillian scratched both horses on their heads, got back into her truck, and drove home to dress for the day. By the time she opened the door, Edgar ran up to her, ready for his breakfast. Jillian obliged him and then made coffee and some instant oatmeal to hold herself together until lunch.

Her one meeting that day was easy. An established client needed to add some successor beneficiaries to her retirement accounts. Although the woman already listed her spouse to receive the account if she passed away, Jillian suggested she also add their children as contingents. The husband and wife loved to travel together, and Jillian wanted to make sure that the children would be protected if something awful happened on a trip. One of the children was married with two children of her own and the other was single. Jillian helped ensure that the contingent's heirs could also inherit their mother's share. When they finished, her client hugged her and told her she was glad to know that her money could be passed down for generations. Jillian smiled to herself and realized statements like those were why she loved her job.

The meeting was over soon, and she dropped by the bank to see if Jennifer was there. Her friend waved her over. "Hey, can I help you with something? I don't want to rush you, but I was headed to Frenchie's Crepes and More. They've only been open about a week."

"I've heard of them, but I haven't tried them yet. I'll miss the pizza place that went out, but Magnolia Hill still has plenty of good places to get a slice or a pie. We've never had a French restaurant," Jillian said.

"Why don't you come with me today?" Jennifer asked. "I'm anxious to try them." She grabbed her black Chanel-style jacket from the back of her office chair. Today's pin was a black witch's hat made out of crystals.

"I don't want to interrupt your plans," Jillian protested.

"I don't have plans, but I need to get back in time for a two o'clock meeting. I want a great lunch now to get me through it." She threw her head back and pretended to snore.

"I'd love to help you get through your afternoon. I'll meet you there in a few minutes," Jillian said.

When she entered Frenchie's, she found herself in a reimagined Paris with wrought iron tables and chairs sitting on tiles fashioned like cobblestones. A large reflection of a slightly askew Eiffel Tower filled one wall, and imitation storefronts decorated the adjoining wall. The painted doors featured signs for "baguettes," "patisseries," "poissons," and "glace." She thought that sounded so much more impressive than bread, pastries, fish, and ice cream.

Jillian selected a table in the corner, where talking would be easier. A waitress wearing a simple pink shirtwaist and pink sneakers came up to the table and laid down a menu.

"Bonjo-ur," she said in three syllables with an accent more from the Red River than the Seine.

"Hello," Jillian answered. "I'm waiting for my friend, but could I get a water?"

"Sure," the waitress responded, seeming glad to be speaking English again. She put down another menu.

In a few minutes, Jennifer entered along with some leaves that blew in around her, compliments of the Oklahoma wind. She looked around at the Parisian façade. "Oh, wow, this is cool."

"It is. I'm glad you suggested it. Maybe Will could find someone to do a feature story on it if the food's good. I'd like to see it thrive."

"Absolutely." Jennifer studied the menu. "I haven't eaten a savory crepe in forever. I think I'm going to order the ones with chicken and mushrooms."

"Those sound delicious, but I think I'm going to try some French onion soup. It originated in France, so I'm still ordering something authentic even though it's popular."

The server arrived soon with the waters, took their orders, and disappeared into the kitchen.

"So, what did you want to talk to me about?" Jennifer asked.

"You know me well enough to know that I wouldn't want to do anything illegal, right?"

"Of course, I do." Jennifer glanced around to be sure

no one overheard them. "But you're making me nervous. What's your question?"

Jillian lowered her voice and leaned across the table, so Jennifer could hear her words. "I've got a question about money laundering."

Chapter Thirty-Three

Jennifer paled and choked hard on her water. Whatever she expected Jillian to say, that wasn't it. She leaned closer before she tried to answer.

"You know I have to be careful how I talk about money laundering. The bank takes security seriously."

For a minute, Jillian's feelings were hurt. Surely, her friend knew that she wasn't going to launder money, herself. Her expression must have given her emotions away because Jennifer quickly spoke again.

"I know you don't want to do anything illegal, Jillian, but I wasn't expecting you to ask that. I am limited in what I can explain, but I'll do what I can."

"I understand," Jillian said. "I learned something yesterday, and I wanted to ask you about it. If someone were getting money from the sale of something illegal, how easy would it be for a bank to catch it?"

Jennifer looked down at the tile-covered tabletop before she answered. "It would depend on how the deposits were made. People have the right to put money in the bank, but if the amounts are large, we have to report them. If you watch television and see conspiracy theory ads, you might think that reporting is a new phenomenon, but it isn't. We've been doing it since 1970."

"Really? The way people carry on, I thought it was

a new practice."

Jennifer shook her head from side to side. "Nope. We increased some of our practices after September 11th, but we've tracked potentially illegal money for decades ahead of that."

"So if someone was selling something illegal…"

Jennifer interrupted. "Like drugs?"

"Like drugs, but not drugs," Jillian hedged. "Still, it's illegal, and they might be making quite a bit of money. How would they put it in the bank?"

"Well, they would need to deposit it in amounts under $10,000. Of course, if the bank sees many transactions that look like someone is trying to skirt that threshold, that will raise suspicions, too. The easiest way to do it would be to bring in more frequent, smaller contributions that corresponded to work they already did. They could inflate the prices to bury the illegal money inside of legitimate purchases."

"So, if I could sell subscriptions for bonus blog content or extended newsletters, I could add illegal money to each subscription before I put it in the bank?"

Jennifer nodded yes.

"I could even use a cash transfer app or credit cards along with cash to move money into my account."

"Yes, that might work, but you would need to be patient and not move too fast. Of course, your other option would be to save up the cash and then buy something expensive with it."

"Like a car?" Jillian asked.

"Like a car," Jennifer agreed.

Jillian's heart sank. Her father would be disappointed that Todd's new sports car would make him more of a suspect. The two women stopped talking as the server approached the table with their lunch. The delicious smell of the onions and beef broth dramatically improved Jillian's mood, and her first bite and stretch of cheese lifted her gloom.

"Wow, this soup is delicious," she exclaimed as she tried to cut the cheese with her spoon.

Jennifer nodded rather than speaking because her mouth was full of food. Jillian watched her swallow. "My crepes are amazing. Do you want a bite?"

"I'm good," Jillian said, "but I'm going to need to bring Will here. He needs to write that article, himself, so he can eat on the newspaper's dime."

"Absolutely. Why did you ask about a car?"

"Did you watch the news last night?"

"I did. You're talking about the guy the police arrested for the murder of your father's friend, aren't you?"

"Maybe. Dad's not sure they've arrested the right person, so I thought I'd see if maybe you knew something that would make Todd look less guilty than he currently does."

"I'm sorry, but buying a car with cash would be a successful way to launder money. The seller might not care where the cash came from or even think to worry about it. When the seller deposited the money in their bank, it would be for a legitimate transaction."

"It makes sense," Jillian said. "Thanks. I appreciate your opinion even if it isn't what my dad wants to hear."

"What kind of car is it?"

"I haven't seen it, and it's second-hand information. I heard about it from Allie, who heard about it from a friend."

"Allie? How is she involved with a car in Spiro?"

"Because of my dad, she knows an archeologist who's also a painter." The waitress came back with two tickets and told them she would take their payment at the table.

"Could the archeologist be wrong?"

"I wouldn't think so, but it's possible. Maybe Dad has seen the car. I'm headed back down there tonight, so I'll ask him. Will and I need to provide a DNA sample to the police."

"Okay." Jennifer sounded concerned.

"It's no big deal. I'm sure we'll be back in Magnolia Hill by tomorrow night. There's too much evidence against this guy. Dad's going to have to accept that a killer lied to him." Jillian signed her bill and put her card back in her purse.

"Tell him I'm sorry about his friend and that I want him to be careful," Jennifer said.

Jillian laid down her spoon in her empty soup bowl with sadness. "I will. Thanks for introducing me to this restaurant. It's awesome. I'm already looking forward to my next meal here."

Chapter Thirty-Four

After lunch, Jillian dropped by Allie's to be sure she didn't want to go back to Spiro. Allie's front yard was decorated with pumpkins and scarecrows, and she had put a small witch's hat on her purple Talavera pottery lizard.

Jillian rang the bell, and Allie and her cat, Chloe, answered the door together.

"Nice surprise. Did you tell me you were stopping by?" Allie smoothed her hair with a green-stained hand. "I was painting the leaves for my sparkly pumpkins."

"No, sweetie, I was in the area, and I wanted to be sure you didn't want to go back to Spiro with me later tonight."

"Do you want me to?" she asked softly. Jillian could hear the fear in her voice.

"No, there's no need. I just didn't want to go without asking."

"I'd rather stay here if you don't mind."

"Not at all." Chloe rubbed up against Jillian's leg, and she bent down to pet the plump, friendly cat. "I'm sure we'll be back by tomorrow, but Edgar was angry with me over his lack of wet food earlier this week. I always leave him with giant bowls of dry food, but he'd love it if you could stop by and feed him."

"And I'd love to feed him, too." Allie picked up

Chloe and scratched her behind her ears. "I like taking care of kitty cats more than running from ancient spirits."

"I'm afraid the spirits were a scam," Jillian said. Unlike Allie, she was disappointed that the blue lights were only a fraud. She was sadder, yet, that the fraud likely led to murder.

"I know, but I prefer staying here. Plus, Ace has some fun Halloween activities planned for us. I like haunted houses when I know the ghosts aren't real. I also need to finish up more pumpkins before Halloween."

"How's your commissioned piece coming along?"

"It's good. I'll make the deadline if I don't get interrupted."

"You mean by blue lights and dead bodies?"

"Something like that. I like to paint in the gallery. The background noise of people working keeps the room from being lonely."

"It sounds like fun."

"It is. And Kandace provides coffee in big carafes. She only charges us a dollar a cup or refill. If she has leftover food from the day before, she gives it to us for free."

"I'm glad she's doing her part to keep the artists from starving. Maybe I should take up painting," Jillian said.

"That she does. Most of us don't make a lot of money from our art. The woman who works beside me paints small watercolors of local sites. She sells them for fifty dollars each."

"I'm surprised they are that inexpensive. Is it the going price?"

Allie sighed. "That depends on so many things. The more people like what you paint, the more you can charge. Of course, I've never been sure what people would like."

"My friends have bought expensive art that I hated." Jillian pointed to a painting on Allie's wall. "Your stuff is better, and I'm not saying that because I like you. I hope you make more than fifty dollars per piece."

"I usually do," Allie admitted, "but I'm not one of the high-earning artists in the studio."

"So you guys talk about what you earn? I've always thought artists didn't care about money. I'm surprised it's a conversation topic."

"I don't think money directs most of what we do, but we like to eat." Allie laughed. "I make good money painting doors and fences, and I do okay selling my pieces. But you know my friend, Char. She makes those cool bowls you always notice at the art shows. She earns more than I do. I don't mind. I've bought her bowls, too."

"I love them," Jillian agreed.

"And Abigail makes the paper with flowers and seeds. She earns great money both in the studio and at any kind of festival."

"I've bought her paper," Jillian said. "It's gorgeous."

"One of the best-selling painters is your dad's friend, Don."

"Really? That's great. I've never seen his work."

"He usually paints Native American styles or themes. Some represent modern life, and some represent earlier periods, like at Spiro."

"That's really cool. The next time we go to an art festival, I need to check out his stuff."

"We should. I saw him yesterday, and we talked about our Halloween plans. He's going to take his grandkids to the community haunted house. I told him that Ace and I should double date with him and his wife." Chloe meowed indignantly.

Jillian laughed. "Chloe's got the right idea. I can't imagine the two of you hanging out with a huge flock of grandchildren. If I remember correctly, he had two or three kids who gave birth to two or three kids apiece. That's nine little kids in a haunted house, Allie. Can you imagine all the screaming? And what if they take off running in different directions? Be careful what you promise."

Allie shot her thousand-watt smile at Jillian. "Yeah, maybe Ace and I will wait and go later. You and Will have fun down in Spiro, but stay safe."

"We will. Thanks for taking care of kitty."

"Don't worry. I'll feed Edgar if you aren't back tomorrow. Let me know. Is Mister's mom feeding Agatha?"

"She is, and she's going to refill Agatha's hole for me if Agatha digs it again."

"So she's still at it?" Allie asked.

"She is, silly girl."

"I bet she's trying to bury something special to her."

"She's a unique horse, but only dogs try to bury their treasures. I don't know. Anyway, I'll let you know what we find out. I'm hoping we'll be back tomorrow. Maybe Will and I can meet you at the haunted house, and I promise we'll come without nine children. They would be scarier than any ghost."

Chapter Thirty-Five

After Jillian got home and pulled out her overnight bag, Edgar immediately jumped inside and flattened himself on the bottom.

"I know, kitty. I'm sorry." She reached into the case to extract him, and he jumped back out and licked the shiny black fur on his back to smooth a rough spot that only he could see.

He glared at her and offered a loud, exaggerated, "Mee-ow." Then, he went to the edge of her case and started pawing at the T-shirts and jeans she had packed.

"You, too?" she asked. "What's the deal with you and Agatha digging?"

Edgar ignored her and continued to burrow into the clothes.

"There's nothing in here for you. Let's go into the kitchen and get you a snack. You can eat while I finish packing."

With Edgar placated by a chunky chicken dinner, Jillian filled her case in no time. She knew she had packed too many items, but she wanted to have extra clothes in case the trip lasted longer than she expected. She didn't want to have to drive into Fort Smith to buy anything.

Finally, late in the afternoon, she swung by Will's home and picked him up. He climbed into the driver's seat and gave her a quick kiss. Her truck was a safer option for them to take to Spiro. A million people drove pick-ups in southeast Oklahoma, but no one else drove a car where every panel was a different color.

Jillian was glad Will wanted to go. The drive, although beautiful, could be lonely, and parts of it were isolated, even though she took the interstate. And she didn't know what was waiting for them when they got back.

Jillian loved talking to Will, even when it was unimportant small talk and details about their days. The trip went quickly, and they were about halfway there when Jillian's phone rang, and her father's smiling image appeared on her screen.

"Hi, Dad. You and Mom should eat because we won't be there in time."

"That's fine, Jilly, but that's not why I'm calling." Her father sounded breathless. "The police let me look at the murder weapon today. It's not real." Jillian's dad choked out the words, and she stared at Will. She was silent so long her father said, "Hello?"

"I'm still here. What do you mean, it's not real?"

"It's not an original artifact. It's an excellent 3-D copy."

"A copy? How could you tell?"

"No one would notice it by looking at it or even quickly lifting it, but the texture wasn't quite right. The coloring, size, and weight were spot on, though. I don't know what to think."

"Wow, I'm glad they showed it to you. Most people wouldn't have noticed. What does it mean?"

"We haven't figured that out yet. I discovered it a couple of hours ago. I would have called sooner, but your mom and I visited Todd's mother late this afternoon."

Will spoke up. "Hi, Robert. I hope y'all were careful."

"We were, son. Right now, everything is so murky."

"We'll be there soon, Dad. We're driving my truck down this time and leaving his car at home."

"Smart," her father said.

"We'll be there within the hour, but Will's right. Be careful, okay?"

"Of course, we will," he assured her too quickly. Jillian thought he listened as well as she did. He continued, "Anyway, we ran into Todd's mother at the police station this morning. She gave me a better insight into how Todd cares about Spiro. She's convinced he didn't kill Fred."

Jillian glanced at Will, rolled her eyes, and sighed. "Of course she is. He's her son. You'd be convinced I hadn't killed someone, too. Isn't that kind of a parent's job?"

"Maybe, but she still told us some interesting things." As her father continued, Jillian's phone connection began to cut out.

"What? Dad? Are you there?"

"I'm here," she barely heard. Then, the phone began to cut out again.

"I'll need to call you back." Jillian picked up her phone and knocked it against the cupholder. "No signal."

A garbled response was all she got.

She realized she was gripping the steering wheel so tightly that her knuckles turned white. She glanced over at Will. "What do you think it means?"

"Well, the old crime reporter in me says that Fred wasn't killed in a fit of passion."

Jillian agreed but wondered how many murders Will actually covered in Magnolia Hill. He continued, "Whoever killed Fred wanted everyone to think the bowl was an original artifact. They took the copy and lured Fred into the woods."

"That doesn't sound like Todd," Jillian said.

"Maybe not, but don't be too quick to eliminate him as a suspect. Maybe Todd didn't kill Fred because of the ghost fraud. Maybe it's something else unrelated to the sightings." Will took off his sunglasses as the eastern sky was beginning to darken.

"But the killer used a 3-D replica of a bowl as the weapon. I don't believe that Todd went to that trouble when he could have simply picked up a rock," Jillian insisted. "Plus, if he really loves Spiro, I can't imagine him believing that an ancient artifact or a copy would be a morally appropriate tool to kill someone with."

"Maybe he was trying to throw everyone off. Remember that most libraries have quite good replicators, although making the copy the same weight as the original was a nice touch. I don't know how easy that is to accomplish at the library."

"But the 3-D replicators at the university would do it," Jillian said softly.

"They would, but why would that matter?"

"Don White's teaching assistant, Harvey, makes 3-D replicas of ancient artifacts for his class. He was excited about bringing the ancient worlds to life. Kandace told me about it before you got there last night."

"Why would he want to kill Fred?"

"I don't know, but there could be half a dozen reasons related to his studies. With the new information, Harvey seems to be as good of a suspect as Todd."

"Maybe," Will said, "but I still think Todd has plenty of motive. Does your phone have any signal yet?"

Jillian glanced at the flat line in the upper corner of her screen. "Not yet. I'll watch for deer, but I'm going to get to Spiro as fast as I can. I'm anxious to hear what Todd's mom thinks."

Chapter Thirty-Six

The next morning, Will, Jillian, and her parents met for breakfast at the same diner they had eaten at earlier. Will and her dad ordered biscuits and gravy, scrambled eggs, and ham, while Jillian and her mom had the pancakes and bacon.

"I called Todd's mother after we talked last night. She spoke to his attorney again yesterday afternoon," her dad said as they waited for the food.

"What were you trying to tell us about her last night?" Jillian asked. "The cell signal got terrible."

"Like I told you earlier, Todd admits to pretending to be the spirit of Spiro, but the police made him hang up before he could explain why."

"Right," Jillian said.

"Todd told Ken Griffin he created glowing blue lights because he believed someone was messing around with the artifacts in the display."

"Did he explain what he meant by 'messing around'?" Jillian asked. They stopped talking as the waitress returned with plates and the coffee pot. After she refilled the mugs, Jillian's father answered her question.

"He claimed when he would make multiple visits, the display artifacts wouldn't be in the same place."

"They were moved inside the display cases?"

"Yes, the labels were still accurate, but the artifacts were moved. He also thought that occasionally, a piece would be missing."

"Marlene said he came regularly," Jillian reminded him as she poured extra syrup on her pancakes.

"That's right. He told Ken that he started coming almost every day to see what would be different."

"Why didn't he tell the police?"

"Tell them what?" Her father took a sip of coffee. "That he thought someone was moving around archeological artifacts?"

"Then why didn't he tell Fred?" Jillian asked.

"He says he did a few days before Fred's death."

Will finished a bite of ham before he spoke. "Do you think that's why Fred asked you to come down?"

"Todd thinks so. He thinks Fred figured out what was going on."

"None of this really explains why Todd started running around in the woods wearing fluorescent blue paint," Will reminded.

"Todd said that the spirits appeared most often when their belongings were being disturbed. His theory ties to the old legends."

"And he thought the artifacts were being disturbed," Jillian reminded them.

"Todd's an odd duck," her dad admitted. "But he thought that the extra attention at Spiro might lead to someone noticing what was happening. I'm sorry I gave his information to the police. I think they've arrested the wrong person."

"Ken is an excellent attorney. If Todd's innocent, I'm sure he'll be able to prove it," Jillian said.

"Still, want to go with me to the Center and ask some

questions?"

"Sure," Jillian and Will agreed together.

"I'd like to go back to the room," Jillian's mother said. "My migraine is back, and I think I need to lie down in a cool, dark place. I'm sorry, but let me know what you uncover."

"I'm sorry, too, Mom. Will you be okay?"

"I will. You guys go figure out who killed Fred."

The drive to the Center was beautiful as the leaves were even more brightly painted than before. A wet summer had kept the foliage from drying up and turning brown, and the trees and hills in southeast Oklahoma made it an autumn destination. Still, Jillian's worries cast a shadow over the otherwise gorgeous scene.

When they arrived at the Center, Marlene was sitting behind the welcome desk. Jillian noticed that security had been increased, and five or six guards stood close to the display cases.

When Marlene saw them, she came around the desk and buried them in giant hugs. "It's so good to see you again," she gushed. Jillian wondered why her spouse would be so ugly toward her. Marlene seemed to have lots of love to give.

"I like it down here," her dad said. "I just don't like the reason I'm here."

"No, none of us do," Marlene admitted. "Can I do anything to help?"

"I wondered if Todd talked to you about anything before Fred was attacked."

"Todd was always talking about something," Marlene complained. "He came by the display all the time. It was almost creepy. I mean, I like archeology more than most people, but Todd was obsessed with it. I guess he finally cracked," she finished.

"So you think he killed Fred?" her father asked.

"Of course. And the police agree with me," she said. "Don't they?"

"Oh, they do," he assured. "I only wondered if you saw anyone else hanging around or behaving strangely."

"No. I mean, recently, we have been juggling more visitors than average. This display has helped our tourist numbers. And I hate to admit it, but the reappearance of the ghost, real or otherwise, boosted our numbers, too."

"I'm sure it did," Will agreed.

"But no, I haven't seen anyone acting strangely or who didn't seem to belong here. It's a small park. I'd recognize a new face."

"Of course you would," Jillian said. "Mind if I look around?"

"No, enjoy the display."

Jillian examined the larger artifacts carefully. If someone were replacing original pieces with 3-D copies, they would focus on the items that would sell for more. She couldn't see anything that distinguished one piece from another. Her dad had walked up beside her. "Can you tell if these pieces are originals or copies?" she asked him.

"Behind the glass and unable to touch them, I can't be sure. I think they would let me handle the artifacts, but I don't want to attract that much attention." They walked farther along the case.

"Dad, I don't think you need to touch anything to spot a problem here," Jillian said, pointing to a label with a ceramic, white cereal bowl displayed behind it.

"What? How did someone do this? Where have they taken the artifact?"

Chapter Thirty-Seven

The police arrived shortly after Jillian discovered that someone had moved an artifact and replaced it with a contemporary, inexpensive proxy. They talked to her and her father, and afterward, Jillian suggested she and her dad walk outside. She thought he looked shaky and pale. Will stayed inside to listen for anything that might give them information they could use.

The warm sun and cool breeze cleared Jillian's mind, and her father looked better after a few minutes. "I wonder if the murder weapon was displayed in the same place as the cereal bowl?" she asked.

"It's the only logical solution," her dad agreed. "You know that means that Fred's murderer has to be someone related to the Center."

"I'm not sure that changes our list of suspects," Jillian said. "Marlene has a key, Suzanne had access to one, and Todd hung around so often he might have seen where someone kept a display key and made a copy of it."

"I know. And don't forget what Kandace told you about Don's teaching assistant, Harvey. Money must be the motive, but it's not easy to find buyers of Mississippian art. The seller would need a few connections or names to throw around."

"Again, that doesn't lower our list of suspects."

"I hate to think that I'm friends with someone capable of murder." Her father's complexion paled again.

"I'm so sorry, Dad," Jillian said. "I can't imagine."

He took in a shaky breath. "And to use the beautiful site and relics of Spiro for a criminal enterprise. How could they?"

"I don't know. Where do you want to go now?"

"I want to talk to Suzanne again. I wonder if she might have remembered something important."

Will caught up with Jillian and her dad outside.

"Did you hear anything interesting?" she asked.

"Not really. The police still seem convinced that Todd was the killer. Marlene admitted she kept the key to the display in her desk drawer. Even though they stepped up security, too many people had access to the artifacts given their value."

"It looks that way." Her dad sighed. "I'm disappointed that Fred didn't keep things more tightly controlled, but I'm sure he thought everyone was trustworthy. Come on, let's try to talk again to Suzanne."

Suzanne was waiting for them on her front porch when they arrived. She had a new pumpkin beside the front door, but she still appeared as haunted as a few days earlier. Jillian couldn't imagine her anguish. Suzanne disappeared into her kitchen and came out with lemonade and cookies from the latest installment of food brought by her friends.

Jillian's father explained the replaced artifact and asked if she knew anything that might help them find the thief and killer.

"Robert, I'm so sorry. I can't remember anything Fred said that worried me. I know he was stressed about the exhibit, and honestly, he was looking forward to it moving to the next venue. You know, even with all the extra security, the Center is small."

"Had Fred met anyone new?" Jillian asked. "An employee, visiting archeologist, anyone?"

"If he did, he didn't tell me, but I'm not sure he would have thought to," Suzanne admitted. Jillian glanced at Will.

Suzanne appeared to notice their exchanged looks. "We didn't keep secrets from each other," she said. "But if Fred didn't think something mattered, or if he knew I didn't know the people involved, he might not have thought to tell me." Suzanne gazed out the window. "I'd give anything for him to tell me something he thought was boring. I miss the sound of his voice."

Jillian didn't know what to say. How could she be questioning Suzanne when she was so obviously distraught? She decided to ask one last question and then leave the woman alone.

"Did you know Todd Block?"

"I did. He was quirky, but he was a nice young man. And he adored Fred. I'm sure he didn't kill him."

"I think the same thing," Jillian's dad said. "Unfortunately, the police don't agree, and we have no great leads for them."

"I know." Suzanne sighed. "But I also know that Fred never suggested that Todd was threatening."

"Okay, by any chance, was Todd into 3-D printing?"

"I wouldn't know. I think he's busy with his podcasting and selling his merch. Isn't that what he calls it?"

"Probably," Jillian said. "Do you think he came from money?"

"Todd? No. He was raised by a single mom and hustled fast food jobs all the way through high school to help with the bills. He knew every meal deal in a fifty-mile radius. He'd go to Fort Smith for half-price tacos and Sallisaw for the buffet special. He even knew the two-for-one coffee promos here in town, along with twenty-five percent off burgers on Mondays at the diner up the road."

"So, he didn't have money?"

"Not that I ever saw."

"Thanks for talking to us again," Jillian's dad said. "I promise Molly and I will stay closer."

"I understand," Suzanne said. "Life gets in the way. Just always make time for each other." She gave them a small smile and a wave, and she went back into her home.

As she got into her truck, Jillian looked over at her dad. "Are you tired?"

"No, what do you want to do?"

"Do you think Todd's mother would talk to me?" Jillian asked.

"I don't know. Let me give her a call. I think she'd want to do anything she could to get her son off the hook."

Chapter Thirty-Eight

After a short drive down the state highway, Will, Jillian, and her dad pulled up in front of an ancient apartment complex. Shingles covered the roof and were installed down the sides of the walls, while dingy, white clapboard trimmed the screen-free windows. Dying weeds grew high in the cracks on the sidewalk that led to the door.

"Are you sure this is where Todd's mother lives?" Jillian asked her dad with concern.

"This is the address she gave me. Do you want Will and me to go to the door first?"

"No, I'm sure it's fine," Jillian said. Still, she was nervous. Upstairs in another unit, someone was peeking around a flimsy, white curtain. When she stared at them, they dropped the drape. *It was probably just some nosy neighbor*, she consoled herself.

When they arrived at the front door, Jillian's dad knocked instead of ringing the worn, plastic bell. Someone lowered the volume of a television and called out that she was coming.

A thin, middle-aged woman opened the door. She was younger than Jillian would have expected. Somehow, in her mind, every mother should be about her mom's age or older. But Jillian remembered that she was likely several years older than Todd, and her mom had not been a young bride. Her mother could easily be ten to fifteen years older than the woman standing in front of her.

"Jenna?" Jillian's father asked.

"Robert? Thanks for coming. And you must be Jillian. Your reputation precedes you," Todd's mother said. Her hair was long, straight, and brown, and she was wearing a floral blouse and jean capris.

"I hope it's good. This is my friend Will." She didn't want to mention that he was a reporter in case it further spooked the frightened-looking woman standing in front of them. "Thanks for talking to us."

"Oh, darlin', no. I'm the one who should be thanking you. I know you see me as a mother who believes her son is innocent, but I promise you that Todd would never kill someone related to the Spiro mounds."

Jenna welcomed them into a dark room that was cool from a window unit that hummed across the room. She lit two table lamps, and Jillian thought she was probably trying to save electricity. Then again, some people like to watch television in the dark. The room was clean, but the furniture was simple and obviously inexpensive. Several pictures of Todd, his mother, and a younger girl sat on the mantel and end tables. Todd hadn't mentioned a girlfriend, but he might have a sister.

She glanced into the kitchen. All the dishes were done, and the floor was clean, but the yellowing linoleum was raised under the scuffed cabinets. A small succulent sat in a pot on the windowsill over the sink. Nothing about the apartment suggested that Jenna had money. She wondered if Todd was hiding his sports car from his mother. That would be a lousy thing to do to a woman who obviously loved him so much.

"I wanted to ask you about Todd's love of Spiro," Jillian said. "Dad told me that he admitted to creating the ghost sightings."

Jenna sighed. "Yes, he did. I know it makes him look guilty. But he told me he did it to draw attention to the site."

"Not to make money for himself?"

"I'm sure he made money from it," Jenna admitted. "But I don't think it was much. Making money wasn't his primary goal. He told me that the spirits always appeared when something was wrong, and he thought there was something going on at the site. He wanted Spiro to move into the spotlight."

"Did he tell you what he thought was happening?" Jillian asked.

"No. He told me he didn't want to accuse someone without proof. He should have said more. Maybe then, he wouldn't be a suspect."

"I wish he would have gone to the police first. Fred might not be dead," Jillian's dad added.

Jillian thought Jenna was telling the truth, but she wasn't convinced the son had been honest with his mother. "He tried to scam us when we talked to him," she grumbled. "He hasn't given me a lot of reasons to trust him."

I know, but I promise you that my boy didn't kill anyone."

"Maybe you know more than you think you do. He told us he didn't like Marlene at the Center. Do you know anyone else he didn't like?" Will asked.

Jenna nodded. "Todd thought it was quite a scandal. He didn't like Marlene because she kept hitting on Fred. Todd loved Fred, and he thought Marlene didn't know when to stop."

"Yeah, he told us something like that, as well. He even suggested that Marlene might have killed Fred," Jillian said.

"I know he lied to you about the ghost, but I know he wasn't lying about that. Maybe he was wrong, but he believed Marlene was the killer." Jenna leaned forward in her chair, and it squeaked from the motion.

"We'll try to get the police to look at her again," Jillian promised. "I've got another question. Do you know if Todd did any 3-D printing? I know that libraries sometimes have creator labs. Have you ever seen him make anything?"

"3-D printing? Never. Todd was too busy running down legends and stories to take up another hobby. The only person I know who makes things using a 3-D printer is Marlene's husband, Jethro."

"What does he use a printer for?"

"He creates dioramas of Civil War battles. He's filled one entire bedroom with scenes circling the room. They're about the size of a model railroad, and what he can't get through hobby shops and websites, he builds with a printer."

"Have you seen them?" Will asked.

"No," Jenna answered, "but Todd has. Jethro was talking about them one day when Todd was at the Center. He invited Todd over. When he came over later that night, Todd thought they were cool and that Jethro was talented. He also thought Marlene hated them. Apparently, she wouldn't even go into the room."

Jillian thought about the rumors of Jethro's abuse she had heard. "I'm not sure Marlene and Jethro had much in common."

Jenna gave a sad smile. "Sometimes, people change after you marry them. Or maybe they were never who you thought they were. Why are you curious about 3-D printing?"

Jillian knew her question had been specific, but she didn't want to tell Jenna the weapon had been manufactured. "I heard the police were asking workers at the Center if they knew anything about it," Jillian said. "I don't know why." She shot her father a sharp look and was relieved when he didn't add more information.

Jillian thought Todd's suspicions, Fred's murder, and the replacement bowl all suggested that the copied artifact was important. Maybe Jethro heard the rumors about Fred and Marlene and decided to steal the ancient bowl, replicate it, and do away with his romantic challenge. His actions not only eliminated his competition but also centered the suspicion around Marlene. Jenna's words brought her back from her musings.

"That day with Jethro is the only day we talked about it," Jenna said. Her eyes filled with tears until they spilled down her cheeks. "Todd was a good boy who grew into a good man. He shouldn't have pretended to be a ghost, but that doesn't make him a killer."

"No, it doesn't," Jillian's dad agreed.

"It'll kill me if he gets convicted of a murder he didn't commit. Please promise me you'll figure this out."

"We'll do the best we can," Jillian promised. "Do you know if Todd's come into any money recently?"

"Todd? No, you must have him confused with someone else. Todd makes decent money through his podcast, but barely enough. He works odd jobs around town, too."

"Okay," Jillian said. "I'll text you my cell number. If you think of anything or have any questions, message me." The woman nodded. When she opened the door for them, the wind blew leaves onto the tile at the doorway.

Back in their car, Jillian's dad paused before he started the engine. "What did you think?"

"I think if Todd has money, Jenna doesn't know about it," Will offered.

"Now the only question is how honest is he with her," Jillian mused. "I'm glad we talked to her. Dad, I think your theory might be right. Maybe Todd's the killer, or maybe he just pulled a stupid joke that blew up in his face. After what Jenna said, I think we need to add Marlene's husband, Jethro, to our list of suspects. Let's head back and see if Mom's migraine is any better.

When the three of them got back to the motel, Will wanted to run by the local paper and see if the reporters knew anything they weren't telling the police. He promised to meet them for dinner in a couple of hours.

Jillian went up to her parents' room for a minute to check on her mom.

"The headache's gone, thank goodness. I only needed a few hours in a cold, dark room," she said.

"Good deal. I'm glad you're better." Her father was searching his pockets and taking the cushion out of the chair. "Dad, what are you looking for?"

"My keys. I think I left them in the car. I'll be right back."

Jillian caught her mother up on everything, including her father's promise to spend more time with Suzanne.

"I'm glad he offered that," her mother said. "I always liked Suzanne and Fred. She's going to need friends more than ever now."

"I know," Jillian said sadly. "Hey, Dad's been gone a long time. Let me go see if I can help him find the keys." She opened the door and cried out. Her father was lying beside his car, and he wasn't moving.

Chapter Thirty-Nine

Jillian and her mother ran to her father's body. Her mother dialed 911 as she ran, so Jillian got there first. Although he lay still, and she thought she saw blood behind his head, she also saw his chest going up and down. He was alive, but she was afraid to touch him. Had someone hit him like they hit Fred?

She glanced around the parking lot, looking for a vehicle with a driver. She thought she saw someone sitting in a black car in the far corner of the lot, but an approaching siren and her mother's crying took her attention.

The fire truck arrived first, and they began to take her father's vitals and assess his injuries. Someone hit him on the back of the head, and one fireman told her that her father was lucky.

Soon, she could hear the screaming ambulance approaching. The paramedics told her mother that usually, very serious injuries were taken to a hospital in a nearby town that had a larger ICU. As Jillian got in her truck, she glanced back at the black car. Maybe the sun had reflected on the seat. She didn't think she saw someone this time.

When she got to the hospital, they let her mother go back, but they asked her to wait in the lobby. She sat down in a blue plastic molded seat and looked around aimlessly. One man coughed in the corner of the room, and a mother held a sleeping baby in a chair under the ceiling-mounted television. A cooking channel blathered on about ways to use dry ice in a spooky dinner.

At the front of the room, a nursing station had Halloween paper cutouts taped to the front and small, 3-D honeycomb paper pumpkins on the counter. Her dad had to be all right. He just had to. Jillian knew her father's attack was related to events at Spiro. What had they uncovered? She wiped the tears from her eyes and texted Will and Allie to let them know what was going on.

They both texted back almost immediately. Allie messaged, —*I'm so sorry. What can I do?*—

Jillian asked if she could help with the Halloween Fest at her office the next day. She knew she wouldn't be back in time to help Katherine hand out candy on Halloween afternoon. The downtown festival started at noon and ended at four. Schools were out for teacher's meetings, so the festival led directly into the fun evening events. Jillian knew that by ten o'clock that night, Magnolia Hill would be on a sugar high. She would rather think about that than her poor father and mother back with the doctors.

Jillian read Will's text next. —*On my way.*—

As she waited for Will, she mindlessly scrolled through social media. Soon, she heard soft footsteps coming down the hall. A nurse wearing orange scrubs with a name tag that read 'Juanita' called out her name. Jillian jumped up and followed her to the back.

"How is he?"

"Cutting out all the medical speak, I'd say lucky." The nurse looked at Jillian with kind, dark eyes. Her black hair was pulled back in a single, shiny braid.

"You're the second person to tell us that," Jillian said nervously.

"He's unconscious, but the x-ray and CT scan didn't show any serious damage. Somehow, the blow didn't fracture his skull. He has a concussion, and we'll monitor swelling and look for internal bleeding, but he's likely going to be fine."

"I'd like it better if you took 'likely' out of the sentence."

The nurse flashed a beautiful smile with perfect, white teeth. "Medical practice. Nothing is certain, but please don't panic."

"Thanks," Jillian said, beginning to breathe again. "I'm in finance. Nothing is certain in my world, either. Now, I know what it feels like."

They reached the room. The door was partially closed, and Juanita pushed it open. Jillian's mother rushed over and grabbed her daughter in a big hug. "Jillian, who did this?"

"I don't know, Mom. It can't be Todd."

"Robert was sure it wasn't him. I guess he's been saying it to other people, also."

"You mean at the Center?"

"Probably. And we know he's told Suzanne."

"Someone didn't want him digging around." Jillian stroked her father's arm as he lay still in the bed. "You're pretty sure he's going to be okay?" she asked the nurse again.

Juanita nodded. "I wouldn't be allowed to give you any promises, but like I said, he was lucky."

Jillian's mother stifled a hysterical laugh. "I always told him he had a hard head. I'm so glad I was right."

Jillian hugged her mom harder. "We both are. What's the plan now?" she asked Juanita.

"The doctor will be in to talk to you in more detail. I'm a nurse practitioner. Still, I'm sure he'll be admitted to the hospital tonight. I suspect it won't be ICU, but that will be the doctor's choice. Let me know if you need anything." She walked out of the room.

Jillian's phone pinged. Will's message simply said, —*Here.*—

"Mom, will you be okay if I go back into the lobby and catch Will up on what's happened?"

"Of course, Jilly. You can get something to eat if you want."

"No way am I leaving you until we know the plan."

"Thanks, but I think we'll be fine. Go let Will know what's going on. Maybe he's got some ideas. We all need to be more careful."

When Jillian went into the lobby, she saw Will and rushed up to him. He hugged her around two large plastic bags he was holding.

"How is Robert?" he asked.

"They think he's going to be okay, but somebody hit him in the head." Jillian wasn't able to stop the tears from flowing down her cheeks. Now that she knew her father was going to live, her emotions overwhelmed her. Will held her close while she cried. Eventually, the rush of stress passed, and she was curious about the warm bags resting on her back.

"What are you holding?"

"I figured you and your mom needed to eat dinner, and I didn't know what you'd want. I bought sandwiches, salads, and fries."

"That's sweet," she said, and Will blushed. "Mom

told me to go eat, but I didn't want to leave her here. I'll go back and get her, and I'll wait with my father while she eats. Then, I'll come out and have something. I don't want to leave her until we're sure what's going on."

Chapter Forty

The next morning, after a sleepless night in a different smokey room, a lumpy bed, and a questionable blanket with cigarette burn holes, Jillian staggered back to the hospital. After she had left the evening before, her father had been admitted to a regular room. Her mother didn't want to leave and promised that she would be fine staying with her dad.

Jillian walked through the emergency room, quieter now than it had been the night before. She went up the elevator and walked most of the length of the hall. She was heartened that her father must be doing well enough that he didn't require constant monitoring. Jillian tapped on the door before she walked into the room. Her father was hooked to an IV and a machine that monitored his vital signs.

Her mother uncurled herself from the green, vinyl recliner and stretched her arms over her head. "Hi, sweetie. I didn't intend for you to come so early."

"I wanted to get you some relief as soon as possible. I know it's hard to sleep at all in a hospital."

"True enough," her mother agreed. "I'm thrilled they're taking such good care of him, but I think someone was in the room every hour. Good thing, too. The call button only seems to work half the time. It sticks."

"That's too bad, but I can go up to the nurse's station. At least by putting him into a regular room, we can stay."

"And it means he's in better shape. If they were worried his injuries were life-threatening, he would be in intensive care." Jillian's mom ran her hand through her shoulder-length hair and stood up. "Are you sure you don't mind staying by yourself?"

"Not at all. I came here, so you could go back to the hotel room. Is he still unconscious?" Jillian's dad lay so still in the bed that it frightened her.

"No. He woke up once in the middle of the night. He recognized me, but he didn't know where he was."

Jillian clapped her hands quietly. "That's great news. When he wakes up again, I'll let you know."

"I appreciate it. I'm going to get a shower and some sleep."

"Grab breakfast, too," Jillian encouraged.

"I'll do it, but I want a shower worse." Her mom offered a thin laugh. "Where's Will?"

"We didn't want to crowd the room, and he wants to look around and ask some questions."

"Tell him to be careful."

"I will, but he wanted me to let you know that he can help you with anything. If you want him near or in your room while you sleep, he promises he'd be happy to sit at the table and get some work done. He brought his laptop with him."

"That's sweet," her mom said. "I'm glad you guys are not only dating but that you're friends. You know, sometimes, both of those things don't happen with the same people."

"I know. I like having Will as a friend most of all.

Sometimes, he's quiet, but he's incredibly kind."

"I'm glad, sweetie. If I need anything, I'll call him. He made sure I had his cell last night while I was eating in the emergency room lobby."

"Yes, please be careful. I thought I saw someone in a dark car in our motel parking lot, but I'm not sure. I was in shock over Dad."

"You be careful, too, Jilly."

"I will, but I think I'll be okay. There are too many people around here for someone to cause trouble."

"That's what I kept telling myself last night. I'll be back this evening unless you need me earlier."

Her mom leaned over the bed and kissed her husband gently on the forehead. "Bye, Robert. I'll be back in just a few hours. Try to wake up, so we can talk about what happened." Her mom choked on her final words, and Jillian gave her a hug and a kiss goodbye and settled into the recliner beside her dad's bed. She reached across the rough white sheets and took his hand. He opened his eyes and smiled, and then he closed them again.

She sat there playing a stupid game on her phone with her left hand for a couple hours until she couldn't stand it any longer. Even though she wouldn't want to be anywhere else, she hated hospital rooms. They smelled funny, the machines looked scary, and everything was uncomfortable. Even though she knew the furniture was vinyl so it could be cleaned, she wondered if she would be able to walk when she finally stood. As the thin, white blanket fell down the back of the recliner for the third time, she didn't know how her mother had managed to get any rest.

She yawned with an open mouth because she was

still holding her father's hand. Lack of sleep was catching up with her, so she slowly texted Will with her left hand. She asked if he had discovered anything, and he replied with a thumbs down.

He went on to write that nobody knew who might want to hurt Fred or her father. They were loved in Spiro as much as they were in Magnolia Hill. People were also frightened because they no longer believed Todd was the murderer. Since he was in custody during her father's attack, someone else was the killer.

Will told her he had also talked to the police, and they said they would want to talk to her father after he was more alert. They hoped he had seen the person who hit him. They also wanted to talk to Jillian's mother about their recent activities, so he took her to the police station and sat with her while she told them all she knew. They had moved from being suspects to victims. He finished by telling her that her mom was safely in her room and finally getting some sleep.

Jillian thanked him for taking care of everything while she sat by her father. With the situation in Spiro as resolved as currently possible, she went over her list of other things she needed to accomplish.

She texted Allie, thanking her for helping with the Halloween Fest. Then, she texted Katherine and apologized for leaving her with 10,000 kids to handle. Fortunately, Jillian had already purchased the many needed bags of candy, and they were piled waist-deep in her conference room. Katherine texted back that Allie had reached out. She and her grandmother, Penny, were going to help her. With the three of them equipped with giant bowls of candy, they should be fine.

The nurse came in to take vitals and draw blood, so

Jillian decided to run down to the cafeteria for lunch. She unfolded her legs and stretched the cramp out of her right arm that she had developed by holding it still on her father for so long.

After she ate a brisket sandwich, coleslaw, and remarkably good potato salad, she went back up to her father's room with two cookies. She sat on the other side, so she could move her right hand. She sprayed her hands with grain alcohol hand sanitizer after touching the elevator buttons and dropped the bottle in her pocket. She would hate hospitals less if they weren't full of sick people, but the grain alcohol she used instead of the purchased liquids gave her confidence. They also didn't break her hands out in a rash like the fragranced sprays. She pulled out her phone, sprayed the surface, and started looking at pictures from the Spiro Center, hoping she would see someone who would trigger an idea.

Unfortunately, the pictures were what she expected to see—shots of the mounds, pictures of archeologists including her father, Fred, and Don, and tons of archeology students. The staff, including Marlene, were featured, and even Todd was in a few shots. She sighed, closed her eyes, and dropped off to sleep.

Her ringing phone woke her up. Allie's waving profile pic greeted her as she answered.

"Allie, what's going on?"

Allie's normally cheery voice was solemn. "I just had the weirdest conversation with Don's wife."

"Weird? How?"

"She came by with her grandkids to trick-or-treat a couple of minutes ago. She was friendly, and she told me Don was sorry to miss the festival, but he was down in Spiro."

"Don's here?" Jillian asked. "Did he say anything about coming here to you?"

"No, not even after he saw the news piece about our finding the body. He never said a word about it. In fact, I thought he was heading to Colorado for a few days to attend a conference."

A cold chill ran down Jillian's spine. "Hey, you've seen Don at the art studio. Have you ever seen his car?"

"Absolutely. He drives a black Honda."

"You're sure?"

"Of course, I am. I've parked next to him several times. His car is simpler than his wife's."

"His wife drives a nice car?"

"A Lexus with all the bells and whistles. She deserves it, though. I think Don can live in his own world a lot of the time. I'm glad he got her a new car."

Jillian's head began to pound, and she tried to keep her voice calm as she asked her next question. "When did he buy it?"

"A couple of months ago. He told me he sold some commissioned paintings for quite a bit of money. I don't know where he worked on them. I never saw them."

"Allie, thanks for taking the time to call and tell me."

"I thought it was odd. Why did he lie about going to Colorado? Do you think he changed his mind, or is he concerned about getting attacked, too?"

"I'm afraid it might be something scarier. I need to hang up and call the police. I'll explain later." She looked briefly at her father's peaceful face. If she was right, Fred's murderer and her father's attacker was a man they knew and trusted.

"Put down your phone," Don White commanded from the doorway.

Chapter Forty-One

Jillian jumped up to face the hospital room door and wished that the call button sitting on her father's blanket worked reliably. Don White wasn't a large man, but he filled the door. He reached under his jacket and pulled out a large wrench.

"Don, what are you doing here?" Jillian asked, hoping somehow Allie misunderstood everything.

"Oh, I think you know," Don said as he approached the bed.

Jillian dropped her hand lower than the mattress and hoped Don didn't notice the movement. She also hoped she knew her phone's virtual keypad well enough that she could dial 911. She started talking loudly, hoping her voice would drown out the operator's.

"I don't. Did you come to visit my father?" she asked. She tried to look confused and hoped Don would buy it. Instead, he began to approach the bed. She hung up the phone from 911 and called Will on speed dial. She hit mute, so Don wouldn't hear it, and she cautiously laid her phone under her father's arm.

"You know I didn't," Don growled. "Why did Fred have to start studying the relics carefully and asking me questions? I was supposed to handle the incoming pieces, not him. He was supposed to archive everything and thank people. If he had just done his job without snooping around, he never would have noticed the substituted pieces. With my painting ability, they were indistinguishable from the originals behind the glass," he declared smugly.

"So you killed Fred," Jillian said more than she asked.

"I had to." Don took a step forward. "Just like I have to kill your father and apparently you, too."

"Are you the one who hit him over the head?"

"He figured out that I was replicating artifacts and selling the originals, like Fred did."

"My dad never suspected it was you." Jillian tried to think of questions to ask, buying time until either Will or the police arrived. She hoped Will could hear the conversation. She wasn't even sure the phone was right side up.

"What do you mean?" Don snarled.

"He figured out that someone created 3-D copies of Spiro relics, but he never suspected you. He thought it might be Marlene's husband Jethro, Todd the podcaster, or your T.A."

"Harvey? Why would he think he was the killer?"

"Because Harvey told us that he liked to replicate artifacts to make history come to life. But Allie told me that your wife said you were in Spiro."

Don was still menacing, but he was no longer approaching her. "Why was your friend talking to my wife?"

"It's the Halloween festival back home, and she brought your grandchildren trick-or-treating to my office. Allie was helping me out by handing out candy since I'm here."

"I don't know why Allie was surprised I was here. I'm an archeologist. Of course, I'm down here looking into the murder of my friend," he said slyly.

"No, you never mentioned anything about that to Allie when she saw you in the gallery. You told her you were going to Colorado. You don't know how often we talk," she said, immediately regretting her words as Don approached the bed again. All the pieces fell into place, and Jillian needed to slow him down until help arrived. She looked down at her father's pale face, drew up all the courage she had, and began to speak.

"You've been selling artifacts and laundering the money through the sale of your paintings, haven't you?" Don's silence was almost confirmation, so Jillian continued. "Allie told me you made an incredible amount of money from your art. That's not common, but it's possible, so no one got suspicious. Allie never saw the latest commissions you claim you sold, and I bet you never painted them."

Don briefly dropped his gaze, so Jillian continued to lay out his crime. "You slowly deposited the money from your stolen artifacts using the sale of fictitious art as a cover. Don, why would you? Money isn't worth what you've done."

Don's surprise caused his arm to drop as he muttered, "You have no idea what it's like not to have money. I'm a good archeologist, but I never got included in the interesting work your father and Fred got to do," he said sullenly. "They became celebrities, well paid for their time, while I kept working. The traveling exhibit was my way to make money off my talent in 3-D printing." He raised the wrench again over his head.

Jillian grabbed the hand sanitizer out of her pocket and sprayed the contents in his face.

As the 180-proof grain alcohol hit his eyes, Don

dropped the wrench and yelled out in pain. Jillian took the opportunity to grab her purse. She hit him a couple of times before he grabbed her arm. He started pulling her across her father's bed, so she ignored her disgust at her idea and bit him as hard as she could.

He yelled again, dropped her arm, and grabbed the wrench off the floor. She threw her body over her father's head and covered her own head with her hands. She squinched her eyes closed and waited for the blow, but instead, she heard a large crash and a terrible curse from Don. She opened her eyes to see him lying on the ground while Will stood over him with a chair. She came around the bed only to see Don stand back up. She doubled her fist and hit him in the face. He fell to the ground again and grabbed his bleeding nose.

Jillian heard footsteps as someone ran up the hall and turned to see two new police officers dashing toward the room. How many police worked in Spiro? At that point, she didn't care.

"Oh, thank goodness my 911 call went through. Officers, we're down here. The man on the floor confessed to murdering Fred Winkler and trying to murder my father."

"She's crazy," Don said. He tried to stand, but he didn't raise the wrench again.

"No, I think she's smart," Will disagreed. "She called me, and I recorded the entire conversation, including your confession."

Don glared at him, drawing his lips to a thin line. When he finally spoke, he only said one word. "Lawyer."

The police listened to Jillian's summary, and when they were finished, Will gave them his cell phone. They promised to return it as soon as they had a copy of the taped conversation.

"Does this mean you can release Todd?"

"He was already almost exonerated after your father's attack," one of the officers explained as he placed handcuffs on Don and began reading him his rights.

"If everything checks out, we will release him soon," the other officer promised.

Suddenly, Jillian heard a soft moan from the bed. "Dad," she exclaimed and turned around.

She watched her father slowly open his eyes. "What's going on?" he asked in a shaky voice.

"You were right," Jillian said. "Todd wasn't the murderer." She didn't want to tell him yet that an old friend tried to kill him. That information could wait. "Boy, it's good to hear your voice. Let me call Mom. She was here all night."

"Why am I in the hospital?"

"You were in the motel parking lot, and someone hit you in the back of the head."

"Who?" he asked as his eyes closed again. Jillian didn't respond.

Chapter Forty-Two

After they left the hospital, Will slipped into the driver's seat of the truck while Jillian snuggled as close as she could to him in her bucket seat. "I'm glad Dad woke up. I know the doctor promised us he would be fine, but I don't think Mom and I were going to believe it until we saw some signs."

"Your dad's cool. He's going to be devastated to learn who hurt him and killed his friend."

"He is," Jillian said sadly. "We'll have to tell him tomorrow, but for now, I want him to rest."

"At least the artifacts are likely to be returned."

"What do you mean?" Jillian asked.

"While you were talking to your dad, I heard Don promise the name of his buyer for a reduced sentence."

"What did the police say?"

"They said they couldn't promise anything, but I'm sure they will get the name. Now, whether or not they reduce one count of murder and two counts of attempted murder," Will paused. "That remains to be seen."

Jillian shivered and snuggled closer. "That's such good news. I know Dad will be relieved. I guess this is one Halloween you'll never forget."

"Not any time soon. This week has been scary," Will admitted.

"I'm glad you were headed up to visit Dad. I was

running out of ideas."

"I'm relieved I was there, too, but please, let's never do that again," Will pleaded.

"I agree. I want to focus on my financial firm, not crime."

"I'm disappointed," Will said, and Jillian glanced at him with a confused look. "I wanted you to focus on me." He smiled and pulled his arm close around her. "You know I'm kidding, sort of. I want you to be amazingly successful."

Jillian smiled at him. "Maybe I can do both."

Suddenly, she sat straight up in her seat. "You know, maybe Agatha gave me clues again."

"What do you mean?" Will asked.

"She kept digging holes. I wonder if she was trying to tell me that the murder of Fred was related to excavated ancient artifacts?"

"Or maybe she just wanted to go back out to her pasture," Will offered.

"Maybe," Jillian conceded. "Hey, because it's Halloween, let's drive over to the Spiro mounds."

"You still want to see ghosts?"

"A girl can hope. Come on. It'll be cool. I know they aren't there, but Halloween seems like the best day to see something if it's possible."

"Okay, we'll swing by on the way to the motel."

Soon, they were pulling into the parking lot of the Visitor's Center. As Jillian climbed out of the truck, she heard an owl hoot in the distance, and she shivered as it reminded her of the night she found Fred. A light wind blew thin clouds across the face of a full moon, and Jillian was less frightened after Will came around the car and took her hand.

"You sure you want to do this?" he asked. "You look nervous, and after the week we've both experienced, I wouldn't blame you."

"No, how often will we be down here this time of year? I'd hate to let the opportunity pass without at least trying," she said. "Come on. Let's go." They crunched through the leaves covering the walking path to the site and crossed the narrow bridge. They barely entered the moonlit lawn in front of Craig Mound when they stopped. They stood at the edge of the clearing and watched.

Jillian heard small steps in the woods and glanced over to see a deer enter the brightly lit opening. It paused, gazed at Jillian and Will, then turned to Craig Mound and stared at the ancient site. Jillian's glance followed the deer.

Above the top of the mound, she saw movement. Something shimmered. The shape of a man came into focus. His face looked painted, like the figure on the site's visitor's sign. But unlike that image, he was made completely out of transparent blue flame. Jillian squeezed Will's hand hard and glanced at him. He, too, was mesmerized by the figure. Jillian watched the spirit grow dimmer, then brighter, then dimmer again. At all times, she could completely see through him. Finally, he grew dazzling bright and gazed directly at Jillian. He nodded his head slowly up and down and then vanished. The quiet mound shone with moonlight, covered in mottled patterns from the shadows of leaves, and the owl hooted again.

The deer quit watching the mound and went back to nibbling tufts of grass in the moonlight. Then, it, too, stared at Jillian for a long moment and walked back into the forest.

Recipes for Financial Success

The Importance of Contingent Beneficiaries

Jillian didn't have to be a financial planner to know that sometimes families experienced unthinkable tragedies when multiple members died at the same time. Many of her clients have Individual Retirement Accounts, sometimes called IRAs, or company retirement accounts including 401(k)s, 403(b)s, SEPs, or SIMPLEs. These types of accounts require that a beneficiary be named when they are opened. The beneficiary would inherit the account when the owner passed away.

Jillian knew it was no surprise that the owner and beneficiary were close—sometimes spouses, friends, or parents and children. As a result, they often went places together, and sometimes, they were in accidents where they were both killed.

The death of the account owner and the beneficiary can create chaos with the account ownership. First, it throws the assets into probate. Probate is a process where a judge determines who should receive the belongings of a person who died. Probate is lengthy and relatively expensive. Probate also follows laws of descent and distribution. In other words, without other information, the judge must give assets to predetermined beneficiaries.

The owners of the accounts could have avoided these issues if they had named contingent beneficiaries when they designated their primary beneficiaries. Contingent beneficiaries inherit the assets if the primary beneficiary is deceased.

Jillian's client listed her spouse as her primary beneficiary, as most clients did. In fact, if a married account owner does not want to list the spouse as the primary beneficiary, that spouse must sign a form stating they know they are not inheriting the money. Jillian suggested the woman also create contingent beneficiaries. The woman agreed and listed her children as the people who should inherit her account if she and her husband had both passed away. If the beneficiary is a minor, additional steps need to be taken, but fortunately, this client's children were all grown.

Jillian's client chose to have her children inherit the assets *per stirpes*, a Latin word meaning "by branch." Jillian explained to her client that if she chose *per stirpes*, she would protect her grandchildren. If one of her children passed away before her client, their children would inherit the money that would have gone to their deceased parent. Jillian's client had two children. If one of them passed away before she did, half of the money would eventually go to their children. Had she not selected *per stirpes*, the money would have been inherited by the remaining child, eliminating the inheritance for some of her grandchildren. The woman didn't want that to happen. By the end of the meeting, Jillian was glad to have helped protect the account for her client, spouse, children, and grandchildren. Fortunately, the client believed her rather than consulting her cat!

How to Recognize Money Laundering

The basic definition of money laundering is easy for Jillian to explain to her clients. Money laundering most simply involves mixing illegal money with legal money to hide its criminal source. The illegal money often comes from the proceeds of illegal transactions, like extortion, drug sales, terrorist activity, or, as Jillian discovered, cash earned from selling stolen goods. Jillian recognized the potential for laundering cash earned from the black market sales of artifacts before she caught the murderer.

When Jillian helps clients open accounts, she explains to them that the questions concerning banking activity and the source of revenue are all an attempt to recognize money laundering. Her client accounts have never led to her being concerned, but by signing the application, they are swearing that the source of money to fund the account is legitimate.

Jillian was surprised when Jennifer explained how banks tracked transactions to monitor potential money laundering. As a business owner, she frequently made deposits greater than $10,000, but she also had copies of checks and invoices to document every penny of it. She could see how some sources of income would be more difficult to explain. She hoped that someday, she would need to advise her friend, Allie, to keep good records of checks larger than ten grand. She was sure her friend would be happy to comply.

Sometimes, clients came into Jillian's office with dubious business propositions they had been offered. Usually, they were an obvious email scam where a foreign prince offered to provide $10,000 to clear foreign funds through the recipient's bank account. The crime behind these messages was identity theft, not money laundering.

More rarely, a client would show an offer similar to those sent from obscure email addresses, except the transaction would happen in person, and the promise of cash was real. In these cases, the payer was willing to turn over a percentage of the cash if the payee would simply deposit the funds in their own account and then withdraw them again. For their trouble, the payee made a profit. This practice is usually money laundering, and it's one of the transactions that can be caught by Jillian's applications if the person gives honest answers.

Most people turn down these offers, knowing they sound funny even if they are not sure why. However, cash can be transferred in many ways. Selling expensive items and accepting cash is a much more common practice. Jillian doesn't suggest that her clients can't take cash, but she does encourage them to use caution. She also recommends that she provide carbon copy or PDF receipts. That way, if authorities ever had any questions, the seller has records.

Another common practice occurs when someone asks another party to falsify a transaction, listing items or services as costing more or less than they did. Sometimes, this practice is money laundering, and other times, it's a tax evasion tool.

Jillian always recommends that clients report financial activity accurately. If they don't, they could be assisting with fraudulent transactions or money laundering. Additionally, if a transaction feels "off," they should cancel the deal or find another way to make it work. She reminds her clients that they can always contact her or another authority. Someone will help them figure out their next steps, whether it's contacting a credit card company, the bank, or even law enforcement.

Meeting Your Financial Goals

Jillian found it strange that Morti wanted to consult spirits and her cat as she made decisions. However, she wasn't surprised that her potential client did not understand basic principles of investing to help her meet her long-term goals. Several times a year, prospective clients, and sometimes even existing ones, sit in her conference room and talk about how they only want to own investments that make money. If the market turned negative, they immediately wanted to sell all their holdings. Unfortunately, she must explain that such a strategy isn't possible.

She begins by reminding her clients that investing in the market requires taking risk. Risk can take many forms, depending on the type of investment. For example, stocks can have business risk, where they lose money because the business is poorly run. Regulatory risk can put them in danger of losing money due to new laws and regulations. Political risk, the risk that political instability leads to market instability, is more common in international investing, while market risk is the risk of a catastrophic event that impacts everything.

Jillian believes the risks in the bond market are more insidious because so many investors have been led to believe that stocks are risky, and bonds are safe. Although that statement is roughly true if she is only looking at the volatility of different types of investments, bonds and bond funds have risks that can lead to unexpectedly poor returns.

The biggest risk faced by bonds is interest rate risk. When interest rates go up, bonds that have lower rates struggle because everyone wants the higher rates. This risk especially impacts bond funds because the bonds are bought and sold inside the funds. If a bond is sold after rates go up, the bond must be sold for a lower price. Both the expectation of the drop along with the actual decline at the sale can lead the bond fund to decline significantly. In fact, Jillian saw a recent market decline brought about by interest rate increases where bond funds dropped more than stock funds. Bonds have other risks, too, but Jillian thinks it's an accomplishment when she helps clients understand that bonds aren't safe.

When Jillian explains these risks to her clients, they often ask what steps they can take to lower the possibility the portfolio will decline. Of course, she explains that what has happened in the past may not happen in the future, but that doesn't mean they can do nothing.

She first encourages them to diversify their holdings. Diversification means holding different kinds of investments. The easiest first step is to buy funds rather than individual holdings. A fund comprised of five hundred large United States companies is going to be less risky than choosing one of those stocks to purchase. Then, she encourages them to buy funds holding different kinds of stocks, like small, large, international, or sectors.

Even though it's less common, Jillian also believes in diversifying bond investments. Choices include government, government agency, corporate, high yield, and international.

Jillian explains to her clients that even after understanding risk and diversifying their investments, they can still lose money. The losses are usually less devastating, however, and with time, the funds are expected to recover. Other issues come into play, but by this point, the clients want a break, so she saves those discussions for future meetings.

A word about the author...

Best-selling author Peggy Doviak started reading the Bobbsey Twins when she was a child. Now, an experienced financial planner who changed careers when a stockbroker exploited her mother, she is realizing her dream of publishing a cozy mystery series. If bakers can solve murders, why can't financial planners? Peggy lives in Oklahoma and is owned by two cats and two horses.

Thank you for purchasing
this publication of The Wild Rose Press, Inc.

For questions or more information
contact us at
info@thewildrosepress.com.

The Wild Rose Press, Inc.
www.thewildrosepress.com